Frances L. Mace

Under Pine and Palm

Frances L. Mace

Under Pine and Palm

ISBN/EAN: 9783743303539

Manufactured in Europe, USA, Canada, Australia, Japa

Cover: Foto ©Andreas Hilbeck / pixelio.de

Manufactured and distributed by brebook publishing software
(www.brebook.com)

Frances L. Mace

Under Pine and Palm

UNDER PINE AND PALM

UNDER PINE AND PALM

BY

FRANCES L. MACE

BOSTON
TICKNOR AND COMPANY
211 Tremont Street
1888

My Father and my Mother.

WHEN first your dear eyes look upon this page,
   Remember not that I am far away, —
Bid all the long years vanish, and look back
To that white cottage where the willows grew
And the pomegranates ripened in the sun;
Where, just below the broad piazza, bloomed
A terrace with the tangled cinnamon rose.
Think of that early home, and me, a child,
Calling your names and running down the stair
Expectant of your praises, as I read
My latest verse to those who loved me best.

There is no change; with every thought of you
Childhood perpetual rules my inmost heart.
Though now you sit beside your evening hearth
Hearing the winds lament of winter near,
And I, on the Pacific's summer shore,
Write beneath spicy branches not akin
To trees my father planted, — yet to-day,
As the last page is folded, my strong love
Bears it across the continent to you;
And at your feet I sit and read once more
My latest verse to those who loved me first.

PREFATORY NOTE.

———◆———

THE Author acknowledges the courtesy of Messrs. Harper and Brothers in granting the use of the following poems which originally appeared in *Harper's Magazine:* "The Kingdom of the Child," "A New-World Legend," "Midsummer on Mt. Desert," "Alcyone," "A Rose of Jericho," and "In the Garden."

CONTENTS.

———◆———

Under the Pine-Tree.

Under the Palm-Tree.

CONTENTS.

UNDER THE PINE-TREE.

UNDER PINE AND PALM.

THE HEART OF KATAHDIN.

I.

KINALO, forest-born, dwelt where the blue Penobscot
    Gathers its mountain brooks and sweeps by the
      Moosehead waters,
Calling aloud to its streams to hasten nor dare to
      linger,
Lest the enchanting lake should lure them to sleep by
      her singing,
Never to waken more. For ages beyond remembrance
This was the grand domain of spirits of wave and wood-
      land.
Mighty their sway and strong the magic they shed
      around them.

There dark Kineo sits on his cliff by the soundless
　　billow,
Yonder the Squaw looks back, forever reproachful and
　　gloomy,
While guarded by leagues of forest from step of human
　　intruder,
Katahdin keeps lonely watch in his stronghold of ice
　　and of granite.

Youngest son of a chief was Kinalo; proud of bearing,
None so light of foot in seeking the eagle's eyrie,
So keen on the track of the moose, so swift and sure
　　with the arrow;
And when in his birch canoe he circled the great lake's
　　waters,
The racing waves laughed long to see him bounding
　　beyond them.
Yet often, like one spellbound, he would pause in a
　　breathless silence,
Heedless of hunter's call or the taunt of his ruder
　　brothers,
For then he heard a voice call "Kinalo!" far above him,
Nearer and nearer floating, a mellow and brook-like
　　accent, —
Then with quick heart-beats he saw a face of wonderful
　　beauty

Glancing out from a cloud, or over the bough of a pine-
    tree;
Just for an instant it shone, then vanished in quivering
    flashes.
Only one other knew this mystery which enthralled
    him, —
The dearest friend of his heart, his sweet child-sister
    Wanona.

Often with her he stood, in the shade of a giant pine-
    tree,
Watching the night come down on the mighty mountain
    Katahdin.
Together they watched the shadows, like foemen
    stealthy and silent,
Creep up the rugged slope and war on the sunlit
    fortress.
Soon was the banner of sunset smitten and torn asunder,
Soon the black tents of darkness covered the cliffs and
    gorges.
Then would Wanona hasten her brother's steps to the
    wigwam,
Saying, "I fear thou wilt meet the beautiful spirit who
    loves thee,
And the kiss of a spirit is death; so the aged women
    have told me."

II.

FAIR as a dream was the morning, rosy with kiss of the
    sun-god,
The buds of April had burst into bloom on the willow
    and maple,
Fresh with dew was the sod, with dim blue violets
    sprinkled,
When Kinalo started forth with bow and feathered
    arrows.
" Stay not long alone in the forest," cried Wanona,
" And go not near the walls of the magic mountain
    Katahdin."

Scarce had he walked a league, when the wildwood path
    ascending
Was covered here and there with patches of snow, still
    hidden
By the dense shade of the trees from the melting touch
    of the sunbeam,
And behold! a small, light track, like the step of a
    child, before him.
Startled at sight so strange, for he left the village
    sleeping,

And no child could wander out unmissed in the early
    daybreak,
He hastened swiftly on, the hunter's instinct awakened.
Was it a fluttering robe which hid in the clustering
    alders?
He gained the thicket, and lo! a little brook laughed
    and babbled.
Now into the open sunlight he came, but his perfect
    vision
Saw where a foot had pressed the delicate moss and
    crushed it,
Saw too a spray of Mayflower broken and dropped by
    the wayside.
On, still on he pressed, nor heeded the flying morn-
    ing;
Often so keen the hunt that he heard quick footsteps
    fleeing,
Now on the crisp light snow, and now on the springy
    mosses.
How he could not tell, but the day had flown un-
    heeded,
Night was falling fast, and a forest unfamiliar
Darkly stood around, while the mournful pines and
    hemlocks
Shook their feathered heads in grave rebuke of his
    presence.

Pausing and looking around dismayed at the coming
    darkness,

Dizzy, as one awakened from an overpowering slumber,

He saw high above him loom the dome of a giant
    mountain,

And knew, by the awe in his heart, he stood at the base
    of Katahdin.

"Father Katahdin!" he sighed, "I must sleep at thy
    feet." Uplifting

His eyes, he saw the moon like a bow, and one star,
    like an arrow

Shot by some heavenly archer, flaming just under the
    crescent.

Did the keen rays pierce his eyes and open his inner
    vision?

For suddenly at his side the gray cliff flashed and
    parted,

And the face he had seen in the clouds was beaming
    and smiling upon him!

Maiden or goddess he knew not. A being of exquisite
    fairness,

Slender and lithe of form and tremulous with quick
    breathing,

As if from his long pursuit she had fled to this friendly
    shelter.

Lustrous her hair with beams, and her robe, of a golden
 texture,
Shimmered with every pulse-beat as if from some inner
 brightness;
All spirit and splendor and fire, she stood there and
 smiled upon him.

III.

WEARY no longer was Kinalo; all his boldness returning,
He stepped through the mountain door, which closed
 with a clang behind him,
Reverberating long, like distant, vanishing thunder.
In a mighty hall he stood: his wild, dark eyes swift
 measured
The height of the rounded dome, with glittering crystals
 lighted,
The depth of the inner space, in arch beyond arch
 extending,
Till lost in a cloudy vista, where flashes of lightning
 were playing.

Far down the hall, on a space slightly raised from the
 floor of the cavern,
Sat an old man fashioning arrows. He was white as
 snow, from the feathers

Which crowned his hoary head, to his moccasins crystal
    beaded.

Pale was his face, his eyes with an icy lustre glittered,

His robe was white like mist, and he sat on a snowy
    bearskin,

While deftly and swiftly his colorless fingers wrought
    on the arrows, —

Each a long eagle-feather with a fiery brilliant pointed.

A moment the young brave stood spellbound by this
    ancient spectre,

Then on his hand he felt a soft electric pressure,

And the maiden led him forward. "I bring you a
    guest, my father,"

She said; and her voice was clear and pleasant like
    raindrops falling.

The old man looked on Kinalo, — looked with a gaze so
    piercing

The youth felt his heart beat loud, in a tumult of awe
    and wonder;

For sphered in those faded eyes were centuries of
    remembrance,

With knowledge of days to come, and of deeds that
    were yet unnumbered.

"The mountain will give thee rest," at last he slowly
    uttered;

"Not the brief midnight sleep thou hast known in the
    lodge of thy father,
Broken with dreams, but rest that will strengthen and
    heal thy spirit."
Then to the Fair One turning: "Light-of-the-Cloud,
    thy brothers
Await thy evening call.   Now hasten the door to
    open,
And send thy flame afar to summon and light them
    homeward."

The Beautiful One obeyed, but slowly, with lingering
    footsteps.
Reaching the cavern's front, still backward at Kinalo
    glancing,
The walls at her touch flew open; a flash of luminous
    splendor
Played for an instant around her.   Thus often at sum-
    mer twilight,
After long hours of heat, the sky in the west is
    brightened
With quivering flames from the unseen fountains of
    light overflowing.

IV.

At once, as the flash disappeared, came a rumble of
thunder,
And with it a clamor of feet and a tumult of voices.
A cloud seemed to burst at the door, and a throng of
young giants,
Dark-browed and warlike of aspect and rude of de-
meanor,
Rushed toward the king of the mountain. But Kinalo,
startled,
Scarce heeded them as they passed, so strangely the
monarch
Changed at the sight of his sons. He rose up majestic
And towered in mysterious height till the dome of the
mountain
Circled his brow like a crown. His cloudy locks
fluttered
Like snow-wreaths in winter storms, and his garments
down falling
Drift upon drift of white seemed to rustle and waver.

"What of our warfare?" he cried; and the giants responded:
"Still is Katahdin the victor and monarch of mountains!

Armed with thy thunders, we met the bold demons of
    ocean,
We warred on the hills by the coast, and the lofty peaks
    inland
Trembled at sound of our coming. Look forth at the
    forests
Riven with bolts from our hands. See the rivers o'er-
    flowing,
The rocks from the mountains let loose, and the raging
    old ocean
Lashing its shores in despair that it could not pur-
    sue us.
Yet while we warred on thy rivals our deeds were of
    blessing, —
We wrested the fetters of ice from the harsh hand of
    Winter,
And opened his prison doors wide for the long-hidden
    grasses.
Though the clouds we rode were heavy with floods and
    darkness,
The sunbeams were trooping behind us, and earth is
    rejoicing."

"Bring forth the feast," cried the king, — "strong
    meat for my heroes!
Feed and rest, my sons, and thou " — to the stranger —

"Take thy place in our midst and be glad till the
    morning!"
He sat on his bearskin again, and it seemed but a
    moment,
So fast the elf-feet flew from an inner chamber,
Ere a board was spread and a warm enticing odor
Floated from smoking meat and from wild red berries.
At a wave of the old king's hand all were seated around
    him;
But Light-of-the-Cloud, at Kinalo's shoulder standing,
Seemed with her eyes to answer his inmost questions.

Kinalo, stirred to the soul with intense admiration,
Scarcely tasted the food, but toward the Fair One
Leaned as he whispered, "Speak to me, Beautiful
    Silence!
Tell me thy name, and the name and race of thy
    kindred."

Over his shoulder she leaned as she answered lowly:
"Katahdin, the mountain king, is my father; the Thunders
My brothers are, and wide is their fame and eternal;
I," — and her eyes gave forth a glittering splendor, —
"I am the Lightning; I open the door of the mountain,
The clouds bear me far and wide, yet sometimes I linger
Even at the door of thy lodge, by the blue Penobscot."

Kinalo, looking deep in her eyes, quick answered:
"Now do I know what spell, what magic has drawn me
Ever with awe yet desire to the kingly mountain.
Was it thy hand that beckoned in evening shadows?
Was it thy face whose smile made the hill-top rosy?
Hast thou not called me by name in the glooms of the
   forest?"

She smiled but motioned to silence; for now the dark
   brothers
On Kinalo turned their cloudy and wondering glances.
"Who is this," they said, "who comes from the world
   of the dying?"
The hunter felt a chill at his heart, but responded
With grave and fearless demeanor: "Lost in the forest,
I called on the name of Katahdin, and scarce had I
   spoken,
When the king of mountains had sent this Fair One to
   meet me.
But why do you speak of my home as the world of the
   dying?"

V.

KATAHDIN, who now with noiseless hand was shaping
The arrows barbed with fire, reached forth, and touching

The young man's eyes, said "Look!" At the touch of
    magic
Kinalo's gaze pierced freely the walls of the mountain,
And the wide world lay unveiled. Lo! the sky was
    darkened
With flocks of birds. Their wings like waves in the
    sunlight
Fluttered and floated aloft; but an unseen arrow
Swift and merciless smote each jubilant singer.
One by one they fell; as the last sank downward,
Others came in a cloud, and these soared and carolled,
And perished in all their joy. With stifled shudder
He turned his face. And now in a boundless forest
Vast herds of beasts were seen. Some roamed majestic,
While others stole through the thicket or hid in the
    jungle;
And as they trampled the sweet luxuriant verdure
He seemed to feel the throb of their savage heart-beats.
But some by the wayside fell and silent perished,
Some slew the weaker, and others struggled fiercely
And fought till each rolled in death on the bloody
    greensward.

He looked again, and behold! a vast procession
On a boundless plain was steadily onward moving;
Little children snatching at wayside blossoms,

Mothers, and strong young men with faces of gladness,
And aged ones who tottering clung to their kindred.
On they went, speaking hopefully to each other;
But in their midst there walked a shadowy being, —
On one by one fell his glance of terrible meaning,
His arrow sped, and low in the dust lay the victim.

Kinalo covered his face.   The hand on his forehead
Was softly pressed, and again the walls shut round him.
"I know, O King! there lies the world of the dying;
But tell me, has death no power in this rocky fastness?
Does he never enter here?"   The white king answered:
" How old is this granite wall?   So old is its monarch.
How long shall this mountain stand?   So long shall my
          children
Rule over storm and cloud in a youth never fading.
Son of a dying race, thou dost tremble and shudder
When thou hast seen but death's shadow; yet I dis-
          cover,
With stronger vision, long lines of unborn nations
Crowding the earth as the birds that clouded the
          heavens.
One by one they rise, grow mighty and daring,
Then die that another may live.   On the tree of ages
Is a blossom many-colored, many-petalled,
And the Redman's leaf is the first to fall and wither."

VI.

" LIGHT-OF-THE-CLOUD," now shouted the loud-voiced
    brothers,
" Summon thy dancing elves and sing us to slumber.
Thou and our father may tell the tales of the ages,
But we will sleep and rest from our long day's labor."
Then the Bright-haired One looked earnestly down the
    cavern;
Though she spoke no word it opened, and airy beings
Gathered around their queen. Their garments were
    tinted
With colors of sunset. Like beautiful clouds they
    hovered
Around her, reflecting the light of her radiant presence,
Then glided, like rainbows embodied, a visible splendor
Of light and of motion, their steps keeping time to her
    singing.

And oh, the song that she sung, the song of the
    Home-land, —
So sweet, so wild, awaking the soul's remembrance
Of life and joy ere its birth in the world of the
    dying!

The land of dim, soft lights and musical voices,
Of hills whose glimmering slopes reached into the
heavens,
Of valleys white with stainless, shadowless blossoms.
Oh, there, when death was yet but a word unspoken,
And love alone was mighty, were spirits mated,
Far, far in the past, in the morning hours of existence.

As she sang, the strong heart of Kinalo surged with
emotion,
And scarce could he wait till the last sweet cadence was
ended.
Then cried he: "O maiden! I too know the song of the
Home-land;
'T is deep in my heart. My people have known it and
loved it,
But lost it forever; the words were too sacred for
mortals.
When yet was no sun and no moon in the high arch of
heaven,
When the stars were our playmates, and taught us their
musical language,
In a twilight divine, oh, there in the mystical Home-
land,
Ere the earth-life was dreamed, my beautiful spirit, I
loved thee!"

Still was the cavern, — the storm-brothers heavily
　　sleeping,
Stretched on the bearskins that covered the darker
　　recesses.
Only the old man bent over the fire-tipped arrows,
Only the Fair One watched softly the young hunter's
　　visage.
Suddenly, lifting his head, said Kinalo boldly:
"Would death forget me too if I tarried with you?
Could I share in the mountain's warfare, the mountain's
　　glory?
And thou, most beautiful one, the Heart of Katahdin,
Wouldst thou love me in years to come as in years
　　forgotten?"

Down at the old man's side fell the half-wrought arrow,
And a smile, like sunshine in winter, lighted his features.
He looked at Light-of-the-Cloud. "Shall he stay?" he
　　questioned.
"He knows the song of our race. His spirit remembers.
Shall I give him to drink of the cup of our youth ever-
　　lasting?"

"Ah! give me your draught of fire!" cried Kinalo,
　　glowing
With new-born passion, and rose up with hasty ardor.

"It is for thy sake, O dear and wonderful maiden!
I will see no more my lodge by the cool Penobscot.
I know thee at last, my own from the dawn of creation!"

With step as light as a rose-leaf's fall she vanished
To the inner cave, but swiftly thence returning,
She bore in her hand a shell. In its rosy chalice
Was a liquid red like blood. To his lips she held it,
And murmured lowly: "Drink this and forget forever
The years of thy human life. Of the strength of the
        mountain,
Its joy, its strife, its victory, take thy portion,
And love me, as I will love thee, my dark-eyed hunter!"

He seized the shell and quaffed in a passionate frenzy.
Red were the drops and like an electric current
Quivered through all his frame. Still shining beside him
He saw the beautiful eyes, and again he lifted
The burning liquid. But ah! he pauses, he listens!
What music, tender and sweet, borne far through the
        forest,
Has pierced to this mountain hall? The lapping of
        waters
He hears, the waves of the strong and beautiful river,
The rustle of growing leaves, the whir of the swallow,
The song and the sigh of life. Now fainter, farther,

3

A voice that is calling to him: "O Kinalo! brother!
Come to thy home once more! Come to Wanona!"

Nature had called to him, pleading and pitiful Nature,
Yearning to win him back from the realm of enchant-
    ment.
Down from his hand fell the cup. "O maiden!" he
    murmured,
"My heart and my life are thine, but once I must leave
    thee;
Must bid farewell to my father beside the blue river,
And soothe the long grief of my sister, the flower-eyed
    Wanona."

Stern grew the face of the king, and the eyes of the
    maiden
Flashed with intenser rays. Deep muttered Katahdin:
"Go, if thou wilt, but brief in the world of the dying
Are the hours of him who has tasted the wine of
    Katahdin."
"Go!" said the Fair One, and waved to the wide-open
    doorway, —
"To-morrow at sunset I come, and thou wilt not for-
    sake me."

VII.

HE stood in the forest, the gray mountain silent behind
    him, —
Stood like one waking from feverish, dream-broken
    slumber.
But oh! the cool breath of the welcoming air of the
    morning,
The whisper and rustle of bird-haunted fir-tree and
    maple!
Soon he sprang forward, and strong grew his tremulous
    footsteps
As homeward he hastened through paths that were dear
    and familiar.
Could this be the world of the dying, — this beautiful
    sunlight,
This musical swell of the songs and responses of
    Nature?
Up there, in the shadowless blue, must be life ever-
    flowing,
And who that had shared to the full this glowing
    existence,
Need fear to die when the Unseen Father should call
    him?

There flowed the river at last, and the noonday splendor
Showed, by its tranquil border, the nestling village.
Weary and faint with fast, he saw before him
The broad-boughed pine and the door of his father's
  dwelling.
But who is this that steps from the open doorway,
Looks on him, gazes, trembles? The eyes are Wanona's,
But the form is a woman's form, and a young child
  follows,
Clinging with sunburnt hands to her garment's border.
It is she! No face in the world could look upon him
With such a depth of longing and love and anguish.
"Speak to me, O Wanona!" the wanderer faltered.
"Why dost thou look with the face of a stranger upon
  me?
Where is my father, whom yesterday I left sleeping?"

"Yesterday!" Stern and dark grew the face of Wanona
As nearer she drew, the frightened child uplifting.
"Speak not our father's name!" she uttered sadly.
"Seven long years he has slept in the forest shadow.
Long did we watch and mourn, but at last he slumbered,
And Gray-Eagle-Feather, thy friend of old, is my husband.
Where hast thou stayed? In what stranger tribe, for-
  getting
Thy father's age, and the grieving heart of Wanona?"

Seven long years! Oh the might of Katahdin's magic!
Slowly he sank down under the ancient pine-tree,
Sadly he scanned the faces that bent above him, —
All were changed, and the years were written upon
    them.
When he had taken food from the hand of Wanona
He told them his story. Then, though they vied in
    kindness,
And strove to win him to enter the lodge of his child-
    hood,
He sadly refused. "I have done with earth," he
    answered;
"I have sat in the halls and drank of the cup of magic.
My world henceforth must be in the heart of Katahdin."

So afternoon burned slowly away in lurid
And brazen splendor. Upon the distant mountain
He gazed with the look Wanona well remembered, —
The look he had worn when the spirit voice first called
    him.
And now a cloud grown suddenly dark was surging
Out of the west. The great pine branches trembled
With conscious terror. At roll of the coming tempest
He waved his hand and smiled on his weeping sister
As one who will smile no more. A blaze of lightning
Dazzled the quivering sky. Through her tears Wanona

Saw the old pine shudder and fall, — saw white arms, gleaming,
Seize upon Kinalo.   Darkness and heavy rainfall
Hid him then from her sight.   The speedy tempest
Fled as it came, and Kinalo's friends, approaching,
Found him lying unscarred by the lightning's kisses
In death's cold sleep.   The flying clouds retreating
Made bare the mountain's brow.   There, rosy and golden,
As if a banner of triumph were flung from the summit,
Glittered the sun's last ray, — a farewell signal.

Frown from thy stronghold, gloomy and proud Katahdin!
Wrap thyself close with unapproachable forests,
And dream of the redman's ancient forgotten worship.
Unchanged thou hast watched their leaf grow sere and wither
From the tree of life.   A race who fears not thy magic
Treads the wild paths of the woods, and on the blue water
Boldly sails, unconscious of olden enchantment.
Yet thou art mighty as silent, and often in summers
Hereafter to blossom, shall strangers gazing upon thee
Feel the spell of thy presence.   Then will they remember
The white old king forever fashioning arrows,

The stormy brothers, the haunting song of the Home-
    land,
And the maid who summoned, with kiss of death, a
    mortal
To share the love hidden deep in the heart of Katahdin.

A NEW–WORLD LEGEND.

OF the many beautiful fancies
    With Indian legend wrought,
The bridal of winds and waters
    Enfolds the happiest thought.
It grew as the forest blossoms,
    Without touch or tint of art, —
A greenwood spray of living truth
    Fresh out of Nature's heart.

In the East, that realm of story
    Where even the gods were born,
Was the fairest of all the wigwams, —
    The Lodgings of the Morn;
Behind its rose-red curtains,
    In his lonely majesty,
Dwelt the viewless one, the Heart of Heaven,
    Soul of the azure sky.

He saw the New World lying
   Barren and drear and cold,
Nor voice nor prayer uplifted
   To the morning's gate of gold.
He spoke, and four strong Brothers
   From his breath had instant birth,
Who came as gods with rushing wings
   To each corner of the earth.

Of keen and boundless vision,
   And swifter than eagles are,
One made his lodge with the daybreak,
   Just under the morning star.
Jewels of glistening amber
   Fastened his garment's fold,
And his head was crowned with tossing plumes
   Yellow as burnished gold.

One flew to the glowing South-land,
   His garments all of red,
And feathers of lurid crimson
   Drooped darkly on his head.
The third to the shore of sunset
   Sped with the dying light,
And his lodge was curtained with ebon shades,
   For the slumber-couch of Night.

The last to the Ice-world hastened,
    The realm of the lord of death;
Snow-white were his strong, keen pinions,
    And pitiless cold his breath.
Then to and fro unceasing,
    Wilder and fiercer still,
Roamed over the earth the four great Winds,
    Each seeking his own rude will.

Then murmured the Heart of Heaven:
    "Though strong these Brothers be,
They cannot ripen the springtime,
    Blossom nor fruit nor tree.
I must give them loving helpers,
    Who with wiser, gentler hand
Shall guide their aimless strength to bring
    New life to the waiting land.

"Come forth, O Falling Water!"
    Then a shining one had birth,
And in bright cascade swift springing
    She took her place on earth.
"Come forth, O Beautiful Water!"
    And the great blue lake was seen,
With dripping lilies lifted up
    On her breast of azure sheen.

"And thou, O Water of Serpents!"
  In sinuous, gliding grace
Went forth the queenly River
  Unto her chosen place.
Then called he the youngest, the fairest,
  "Step softly, Water of Birds!"
And the silver-footed Brook stole out
  Singing songs that had no words.

Ah! wondering, rejoicing
  Were the fierce Brothers four.
The North-wind sung his greeting
  Close to the blue lake's shore;
The East-wind's trumpet music
  With the Cataract's voice was blent,
And the West-wind down the river's tide
  His passionate sighing sent.

Long under the forest branches,
  Swift-footed, playful, shy,
Fair Water of Birds evaded
  The South-wind's ardent sigh;
But he gave her the wildwood roses
  And violets for her wreath,
And a whisper at last of sweet response
  Stole on her perfumed breath.

Glad was the watching Father,
   The Soul of the bending sky,
When he saw this happy wooing
   From his hidden lodge on high.
The cloud-birds clapped their pinions
   Loud over crag and plain,
And the bright wine poured for the bridal cheer
   Was the bounteous, sparkling rain.

Now ever in happy union
   The Winds and the Waters live;
Blossom and fruit and harvest
   And the wealth of the maize they give;
And when from invisible beakers
   Dashes the midsummer rain,
They are keeping the feast of their bridal day
   With the wine of Heaven again.

HOW GLOOSKAP BROUGHT THE SUMMER.

I.

OF the old days, of the dawn-days,
    Still the wonder-tale is told
In the shadow of Katahdin,
    Where the master dwelt of old, —
The great Glooskap, the Algonquin,
    Chief of warriors true and bold.

Long had Winter, strong magician,
    Bound in icy chains the land;
Though the wise men prayed and fasted,
    Yet he lifted not his hand.
But he said, " Lead forth a warrior
    Who my magic can withstand !

" Let him find my secret wigwam,
    Face to face and without fear
Feel the power of my enchantment;
    If he bear the burden drear,
I am vanquished, and another
    Shall be found to rule the year."

Dire the trouble of the chieftains;
    Who that midnight path could trace?
Then spake Glooskap: " Thrice at daybreak
    In my dreams a shining face
Smiled and called me. I will follow,
    Even to Winter's hiding-place."

In his frozen lodge sat Winter,
    Fierce and famine-eyed and old,
Giant of forgotten ages,
    Scarred with battles manifold;
On his cruel deeds he pondered
    In the darkness and the cold.

Suddenly the great white bearskin
    Was uplifted from his door,
And one entered, — rushing by him
    Entered too the storm's wild roar, —
And the heart of Winter trembled
    With a dread unknown before.

Strong and beautiful the stranger
 Stood within the darkened tent;
The faint firelight to his figure
 Shadowy grace and stature lent,
And his glances free and fearless
 On the giant's face were bent.

Strangely stirred the heart of Winter,
 Heart of ice within his breast;
But he murmured, guileful ever,
 " Sit within the lodge and rest.
Long thy journey; in the morning
 Shall thy purpose be confessed."

Then the terrible frost-spirits,
 Hastening to their monarch's aid,
Of the gleaming, white aurora
 Phantom fire of welcome made,
And the pipe of cloud and ashes
 In the stranger's hand was laid.

And his heavy eyes were lifted
 With a fixed, unconscious gaze,
While the white lips of old Winter
 Muttered of the ancient days, —
With wind-voices and storm-voices
 Chanted wild and awful lays.

Listening, dreaming, with the magic
   Of the place around him cast,
Soon in chains of icy numbness
   All his senses were made fast,
And the hope of the Algonquins
   Bound and helpless lay at last.

Days and months he slept, yet often
   In his slumber stirred with pain;
Lo! the shining face still gleaming
   Far o'er midnight's frozen plain!
Then with fierce and breathless struggle
   Burst he from the demon chain.

Up he rose to height majestic,
   Taller, fairer than before;
As he rent, in sudden fury,
   The white bearskin from the door,
A long shaft of yellow sunshine
   Flashed upon the icy floor!

" I have tried thy power, O giant,
   To thy dark words listened well;
Now the vision of the daybreak
   Calls me with a mightier spell.
Soon it will be *thine* to listen,
   Mine the wizard tale to tell."

II.

OH fast and far sped Glooskap,
　With shoes of magic shod!
Past icy crag and mountain
　By wonder-paths he trod,
Until his feet sank lightly
　Upon a violet sod,

And fairyland before him
　Its gates wide open threw,
While myriad silver bugles
　From waving tree-tops blew,
For all the elfin singers
　At once the master knew;

And in their midst a being
　All beauty, smiles, and light,
The fair dream-face that led him
　Along the waste of night.
Like morning robed in roses
　She beamed upon his sight.

4

But for no soft entreaty
    The eager master stayed,
"The dark world waits thy coming!"
    He uttered. "Radiant maid,
Take now thy earthly kingdom;
    Too long thou hast delayed."

He caught her to his bosom,
    And fast again he sped,
But craftily behind him
    He tossed a magic thread,
And all the fairy kingdom
    In captive train was led.

The birds flew close above them,
    And filled the air with song;
The golden-armored sunbeams,
    Their escort, marched along,
And leaf and bud and blossom
    And rivulet swelled the throng.

Upon a cliff gigantic,
    By ocean's stormy shore,
High perched the great wind-eagle
    And urged the tempests' roar.
His wings drooped as they passed him,
    And ocean raged no more.

And over old Katahdin,
  Where thunders have their home,
One footprint of sweet summer
  Let loose the spirits dumb.
The lightnings gleamed, the thunders
  Spake deep, " *The hour is come!* "

Into the frozen wigwam
  There fell a flood of light;
In stepped the great Algonquin,
  With visage bold and bright,
And with him royal Summer
  Resplendent to the sight.

Then, smiling, the enchantress,
  With singing low and sweet,
Let fall the pearly mayflower
  Before the giant's feet.
Alas! in that one moment
  His conquest was complete.

With eyes that swam and melted,
  With heart that throbbed and burned,
A gaze of hopeless worship
  Upon her face he turned.
Though slain by those soft glances,
  For every look he yearned.

The wigwam sank about him,
  The blue sky blazed and shone;
The weeping frost-elves, fleeing,
  Stayed not to hear his moan:
"I die for thee, O Summer!
  The world is thine alone."

Oh, in her hour of triumph
  Had Summer been less sweet,
Nor viewed with sudden pity
  The tyrant at her feet,
Her reign had been eternal,
  Our joy had been complete!

But on the humbled monarch
  Dear Summer looked and sighed;
Some tears let fall, — the dewdrops
  Were sprinkled far and wide.
She smiled again, — a rainbow
  The hill-tops glorified.

"Farewell!" cried laughing Glooskap,
  "My warriors call for me!
Dream deep, O fallen giant,
  Till love shall set thee free.
Thy fairy bride forever
  Will share the throne with thee!"

MIDSUMMER ON MOUNT DESERT.

I. FLYING MOUNTAIN.

THE craggy height is won! O smiling sea,
   How tranquilly upon thy lulling breast
The islands dream! We too with Memory
     Will muse awhile and rest.

St. Savior's Valley, bright with morning dew,
   Low at our feet in waking beauty glows,
Its borders tinted with the sea-shell hue
     Of the wild wayside rose.

The tide flows inland; not a sound is heard;
   No whirl of worldly tumult here is known;
Hither across the wave the ocean bird
     Flies homeward and alone.

Twice has the century-plant its ripened flower
   Opened and scattered on this breezy crag,
And full again its blossom, since the hour
      When France her lily flag

Flung o'er these unknown waters. Wild with glee
   The sailors moored, and vowed to roam no more;
But *three*, in priestly vestments, reverently
      Knelt as they touched the shore.

To them the grandeur of the mountain isle
   Had but one meaning, woke but one desire, —
To speed the hour when all these heights should smile
      Upon their altar fire.

A cross of rude device was planted here,
   The first uplifted on New England's shore,
And " Gloria in excelsis " floated clear
      The wondering woodlands o'er.

Brief was the sojourn of these pilgrims brave,
   Patient in toil, content to pray and wait;
For riding fast upon the troubled wave
      Came Argall's ship of fate!

A sudden rain of fire, the swift advance
　Of gleaming arms upon a helpless band,
And cross of Rome and flowery flag of France
　　Fell 'neath the Briton's hand.

No sign remains.　The dew-bespangled moss
　Safe in its breast the burial secret keeps;
But on this plain, beneath his shattered cross,
　　Du Thet, the gallant, sleeps.

Soldier and priest!　From Flying Mountain's height
　We render homage to a sacred spot:
Thine the first grave in all this valley bright,
　　The last to be forgot.

Fall softly, blossoms of the century-tree!
　Long would we keep our isle's historic fame;
Teach thy blue waves to whisper, faithful sea,
　　St. Savior's ancient name.

II. THE SEA-WALL.

NOT always Summer rules the isle,
  Though here her chosen kingdom be;
Against this surf-beat wall has warred
  A wild and angry sea.

For when, in days of old, arose
  Fresh from the deep this wave-washed pile,
Down from his throne of mountains looked
  The Genius of the Isle,

And bade his Titans, ocean born,
  These strong abutments bring from far,
Against the demons of the storm
  To build a mighty bar.

Then wrathfully the ocean rose;
  His gathered waves with sullen roar
Unbroken over leagues of space
  Came thundering to the shore.

Again, again, with clouds of foam,
  White flying banners in his wake,
He smote upon the grand sea-wall;
    He stormed, but could not break.

And still the fisher furls his sail,
  And hides from breaker and from rock,
When in his hours of wrath the sea
    Renews the ancient shock.

For wrecks are scattered in his path
  Like leaves in the autumnal gale,
And pallid faces drift to shore
    Whose dumb lips tell no tale.

But while the tide shall come and go,
  While tempests rage and sunbeams smile,
Safe guarded by its giant wall
    Shall bloom the Mountain Isle.

III. MERMAID'S CAVE.

O RUSHING wave,
Flow past the seaward cliff, the broken shore,
And in the deep recesses of the cave
Call the sea-nymphs once more!

Is it so long
Since here they sat, with pearl and amber wreathed,
And to the sea, that loved them well, a song
Of kindred rapture breathed?

A thousand years!
But what is that to ocean's memory?
Still from the cliff drop slow the misty tears
Of the unchanging sea.

Still ebb and flow,
Seeking and calling with perpetual moan,
Though only sea-flowers in the twilight glow,
And give no answering tone!

With every breeze
Send forth a message, southward, westward blown;
Tell them pink-petalled, bright anemones
Have in their footprints grown.

And some soft day
Of rich midsummer may the wanderers bring,
In this dim grotto evermore to stay,
Beloved of Ocean's King.

IV. BAR HARBOR.

THE island city glitters on the bay,
Pride of the summer sea,
And sky and wave exultant homage pay
Her blooming royalty.

The harbor gleams with myriad snowy sail
That wait her queenly will;
She wraps the mist about her like a veil,
And every oar is still.

But as the sun outpours his ardent ray,
    Afar her beauties show;
Bright awnings, snowy tents, pavilions gay,
    With life and lustre glow.

No hiding-place is this for mournful fate,
    No sorrow here is guest;
These summer palaces are dedicate
    To pleasure and to rest.

Here Fashion plumes her brilliant, airy wing,
    And brightens sea and shore, —
A rainbow-colored, transitory thing,
    Now here, now seen no more.

Pleased with the brief, exotic revelry
    Of this ephemeral train,
In proud delight the city of the sea
    Assumes imperial reign;

While in his solitude, serene and high,
    The Island Genius sits,
Unconscious of the rose-winged butterfly
    Which o'er his footstool flits.

V. EAGLE LAKE.

FAR up the slope, by mountain breezes fanned,
  This shining silver cup,
As if to some great spirit's beckoning hand,
  The hills have lifted up.

Down the bright wave the shadows come and go,
  The answering ripples stir;
Drifting we watch, in gorge and glen below,
  Dark woods of pine and fir;

We lift our eyes, and high above us tower
  Turrets of barren rock, —
Gray, massive heights where foliage and flower
  Shrink from the tempest's shock.

How long this fair expanse, so beauteous still,
  Only the eagle knew,
When to his eyrie on yon frowning hill
  With eager cry he flew!

How long the Indian's stealthy pathway led
  Up from the island shore,
And though the wild-eyed deer before him fled,
  He paused to gaze once more!

Yet as to-day we dip the gleaming oar,
  And gayly float along,
While happy voices from the farther shore
  Hail us with shout and song,

As fresh, as full with dew of forest rills
  This silver mountain cup,
As when to some great spirit of the hills
  It first was lifted up.

VI. SUNRISE ON GREEN MOUNTAIN.

A PALE gray light, a single line of rose,
  Reveals where Night and Dawn
Are scattering blossoms at the orient shrine
  Of the approaching morn.
The mountain-tops below this utmost height
Are still in shadow; in the vale 't is night.

Afar the ocean slumbers, and it seems
    Upon its tranquil breast
To clasp its islands, lulled last night to sleep,
    In morning's sweeter rest.
For leagues away the sea is silent, save
Where island shores feel the caressing wave.

But from the forest hills which circle round,
    A long, low bugle-note
From the white-throated sparrow of the woods
    Begins to swell and float;
Bird answers bird; the music soars until
The mountains with their matin chorus thrill.

Now Nature scarcely breathes. A mellow glow,
    Broader, intenser, higher,
Flushes the eastern world from zone to zone,
    And — are the clouds on fire?
For suddenly a dazzling splendor lights
The outer edges of yon heavenly heights.

It is the signal-fire! The lower land,
    Hushed and unconscious still,
Delays its worship till the coming sun
    Salutes the monarch hill.
Awake, ye valleys! lift the jubilant lay!
For on the mountain-top I speak alone with day!

VII. ECHO LAKE.

In sunset beauty lies the lake,
  A limpid, lustrous splendor!
The mists which wrapped the mountain break,
And Storm Cliff's rugged outlines take
  An aspect warm and tender.

Now listen! for a spirit dwells
High in these mountain nooks and dells.
      Echo!   *Echo !*
      Hail to thee!   *Hail to thee !*

Sad Echo, mocked of all her kind,
  Here haunts the fleeting summer,
And sends her voice upon the wind,
Still hoping long lost-love to find
  In every transient comer.

Not where 'mid silver beeches shines
  The lake's pellucid fountain,
But high o'er tangled shrubs and vines
She dwells amid the spectral pines,
  The spectre of the mountain.

Float nearer still and drop the oar,
  Here where the lilies glisten;
O Echo, we return no more;
For us beyond the island shore
  True love doth long and listen.

Thou grievest not, nor dost rejoice,
O wandering, solitary Voice!

      Echo!   *Echo!*
      Farewell!   *Farewell!*

AT SILVER LAKE.

WOULD you feed on the strength of the hills, —
Would you drink of the wine
That is poured from the balsamic boughs
Of fir-tree and pine?
Then into the wilderness come
And the feast partake,
While you linger and rest on the shore
Of fair Silver Lake.

The beautiful hills stand near;
At daybreak you see
The mists that have slept all night
Under cliff and tree;
And all day on the high green slopes
The sun is at play
With the shadows that stealthily creep
In his royal way.

Warm and rich is the light
  On the valleys poured,
Urging to verdure profuse
  The odorous sward;
And pure and keen is the air
  From the mountains brought,
With the life of their iron springs
  Abundant fraught.

Not by the loud-voiced sea
  Is such deep repose;
Not on the briny winds
  Such healing flows;
Nature her own haunt makes
  In the still, green wood,
And the touch of her hand bestows
  But in solitude.

Long and sweet are the hours,
  And when night grows deep,
The waters with lullaby rare
  Shall sing you to sleep;
Shall soothe you with musical dreams,
  Till at dawn you awake
To find a new day looking love
  On fair Silver Lake.

WELCOME HOME.

Read at the unveiling of the Westminster Abbey bust of Longfellow, at Portland, Me. Feb., 27, 1885.

FACE of our Bard Beloved! clothed upon
　With an immortal beauty, welcome home!
Bringing the crown in song's dominion won,
　To the dear city of thy boyhood, come!
Though now no more the wind from off the sea
Shall bring the "long, long thoughts of youth" to thee.

Loyal and fond thy heart to us was turned
　From prouder seats of honor and renown;
Through shadowing years thy memory still discerned
　The haunts and faces of the seaside town.
And we, though round the world thy songs had flown,
Rejoiced to know the minstrel was our own.

From yonder waves that moan along the bay,
   From yonder woods that whisper of thy fame,
Awoke the themes of many a soaring lay
   Whose wings, unfurled, were dipped in sunrise flame.
Here Nature taught thee her serenest truth,
And gave thy soul to drink of deathless youth.

Sovereign of hearts! It was thy heritage
   A rare and happy realm to have and hold;
Magician! bringing forth from every age
   Treasures, time-worn, and changing them to gold;
Priest! at the altar of the world's delight,
With garments beautiful and always white.

For shone abroad thy fair and full-orbed life
   With the still radiance of a morning star,
And fell thy songs, on days of cloud and strife,
   Like bells of peace rung clearly from afar;
The latest cadence wafted on the air,
Thy life's Amen, — "*'T is daybreak everywhere!*"

Oh, well may generous England give a place
   To thee among her sons of song sublime!
No purer life that haunted shrine shall grace,
   No sweeter voice ring down the aisles of time.
Yet we, with tenderer worship, lift above
Thy laurels the undying rose of love.

THE HARVEST OF LILIES.

To the angel of light who stands nearest,
    Illumined by rays from the throne,
Who bears forth His messages dearest,
    When He comforts and strengthens His own,
Speaks the Saviour, — "The Easter bells ringing
    Waft echoes that reach to the sky;
From gardens of bloom, freshly springing,
    Bring flowers for my Temple on high!"

Then the angel, with wings of white splendor,
    Speeds far through the song-sounding land,
And he gathers the flowers pure and tender
    Which April uplifts in her hand.
He lingers by chancel and altar
    Where the souls of the lilies arise;
Then with pinions that stay not nor falter
    He bears them with joy to the skies.

" Dear flowers! of my earth-life a token,
   Remembrance most precious they bring
Of the hour, when, the death-slumber broken,
   Every bud woke to welcome its king.
But from hearts yet unsullied by sadness
   Steal perfumes far sweeter above;
From lips warm with praises and gladness,
   Go gather the lilies of Love! "

In wonder, yet swiftly and lightly,
   He stoops once again to the earth;
And behold! the blest flowers springing brightly
   Where joy and affection have birth.
Unseen, but of sweetness immortal,
   In warm, grateful hearts they unfold;
And the angel bears back to Heaven's portal
   Rose-petals with chalice of gold.

"Go once more, and be sorrow's evangel!
   There are graves where the desolate grieve,
Through tears that would blind thee, O angel!
   There are some who adore and believe.
There are spirits in anguish victorious,
   There are hopes which no warfare can scathe,
Most fragrant and starlike and glorious, —
   Go, bring me the lilies of Faith! "

A moment is stillness in Heaven,
 For woe is a mystery there,
And trust, to the sorrowing given,
 They need not who cannot despair.
But when, from the winged one returning,
 Christ presses these flowers to His breast,
Heaven's shrine with fresh incense is burning,
 And Easter is shared by the Blest!

MOTHERLESS.

I SAW two song-birds in the spring
   Nest-building in the elm-tree's shade, —
Ah, shrill and sweet their music through the glade!
   For life is such a joyous thing
   When birds are building in the spring.

And later, when the dawns were long,
   At earliest break of day I heard
The call of nestlings and of mother-bird.
   The boughs were full of scent and song,
   And love their theme the whole day long.

But what swift gleam of happier state,
   What luring voice of sky or star
Suddenly bade the mother soar afar,
   Leaving on wind-rocked boughs her mate
   And songless birdlings desolate?

Oh, who can know her skyward quest?
Yet is she fled, and evermore
She sings apart upon an unknown shore.
O mother-bird!   O broken nest!
O storm-clouds hanging in the west!

THE MORNING SONG.

REJOICE, O world, rejoice!
    Some magic among the trees
Is touching a thousand musical keys,
And the morning has found a voice.

The robins are come again
With tender, melodious note;
The blue-bird trills from his delicate throat
A music like summer rain.

From the field by the river's brink,
Where violets hide his nest,
Soars high with a canticle of the blest
The jubilant bobolink;

And the golden oriole,
In the snow-white apple boughs,
Pours his rich note and singing glows
Like a flower that has found a soul!

Swallow and sparrow are glad;
The very skies of May
Are thrilling with sound at break of day,
And the young Year, music-mad,

In flowers his tribute pays, —
Purple and white and rose,
While forth from the beautiful bird-choir flows
The rapture of Nature's praise.

NOT OF THE WORLD.

I OFTEN think that God loves best the flowers
    Which bloom for Him alone, which are not seen
By worldly eyes, nor plucked for worldly bowers, —
    Stars of the wildwood, lustrous and serene.

Fair in His sight may be the victor rose
    Which bursts in bloom the hero's hour to greet,
And dear the purple amaranth which grows
    Spontaneous underneath His singers' feet;

But the lone violet which for love's own sake
    Its life exhales in pure, unconscious good,
Some sunless glen a glowing shrine to make,
    With urn of incense in the solitude, —

Not with the greenwood roof its sweetness ends,
    Though moss and mould hold close the slender spire;
Warmly the Heart of Heaven above it bends,
    And a new note thrills Nature's answering lyre.

THE MISTAKE OF THE FAIRIES.

A ROVING child
　　Once fell sleep within a fairies' ring.
It was in June, when many a viewless thing
Has breath and motion in the breezes mild;
When every leaf conceals a fluttering wing,
As at their blossom-work the thronging fairies sing.

　　　The startled fays,
Suddenly hindered in their sweet employ,
Circled around the fair, unconscious boy,
With quick resentment in their sparkling gaze.
Yet now within their ring one boon of joy
They must bestow, one gift without alloy.

　　　Then each in turn
Spoke hastily, her largess to deny;
Wealth, Beauty, Power, and Pomp unkindly cry,
" For our rich bounty vainly shall he yearn!"
Love pitying looked, but slowly passed him by, —
Poor infant! in his sleep he stirred and breathed a sigh.

At last the queen
Bent o'er his fragrant locks and lingered long
To see how rosily he slept among
The wrathful fairies, helpless but serene.
"Wake, child!" she said. "I would not do thee
    wrong,
But I can only grant the simple gift of song."

O queen unwise!
Unwitting of the mischief thou hast done,
No finer charm was yet by fairies spun,
Opening all treasure to his waking eyes.
What good is hid from him, beneath the sun,
Who in this magic power the world itself has won?

A SWEDISH DRINKING–HORN.

L OOK on this Drinking-horn,
    Brought from old Norseland,
Here amid trophies
    Of other days placed ;
It stands upon silver feet
Wrought well and quaintly,
Its broad lid of silver
    Heavily chased.

Grand was the wassail,
When first this beaker,
Foaming with yellow mead,
    Passed round the board ;
Loud rang the voices
Of bard and of chieftain,
When to the mighty names
    Freely they poured.

Or when the midnight
Beamed like the morning,
And minstrels sat watching
    The midsummer out,
The rosy hours ringing
With praises of Baldur,
This lordly cup passed with
    The song and the shout.

Now in a stately
And beautiful chamber,
Rich in the treasures
    The scholar holds dear,
Relic of ages past,
Stands the old Drinking-horn,
Empty of vintage
    And silent of cheer.

Yet call it not empty!
Over the shining lid
Leap wordless echoes
    Of revel from far ;
Icelandic saga
And skald-song of Sweden,
And Hail of the Vikings
    Home-coming from war !

It rings with the clangor
Of songs that are ended,
It sparkles with splendor
　　Of festivals fled!
Oh, touch it lightly
With reverent fingers, —
It brims with the wonderful
　　Wine of the Dead!

MY INDIAN SISTER.

ON my threshold yesterday,
　　Like the April morning smiling,
Stood a dark-eyed Indian dame,
　　With soft speech my ear beguiling.

Baskets of all hues she showed,
　　Blue, gold, red, in rainbow order,
Woven of sweet-scented grass
　　From Old Orchard's ocean border.

"Buy them, sister?"　One by one,
　　With a loving touch she fingered;
I, with little basket lore,
　　Charmed by her sweet accents, lingered.

While she told their use and worth,
　In her face I read her story, —
Simple fulness of content,
　Unaware of worldly glory.

In the winter snugly housed
　On Penobscot's white-walled island;
Tenting free in summer days
　By sea beach and airy highland;

Fire beneath the greenwood-tree
　Lighting all her loved ones' faces, —
What cared she that deeds of fame
　Stirred the world in far-off places?

Was I sure that fortune's boons
　Best and happiest had missed her, —
This strong, smiling one who looked
　In my eyes and called me "sister"?

All that to my life would come
　As its best and brightest guerdon,
On her simple soul would lay
　An unutterable burden.

Of her store I took at last
  A gay blue and crimson treasure,
Lightly wondering which had given
  To the other greater pleasure.

Some day I may greet again
  Her glad face, beyond the River;
Near of kin we there may be:
  Good-by " sister," — not forever.

BY THE PISCATAQUIS.

IN the gray wintry morning
 I woke to hear the fall
Of the river over the milldam,
 With the old familiar call, —

The hoarse and muffled murmur,
 Solemn and deep and strong,
Which lulled my childhood's slumber
 And grew into my song.

Now, after years returning,
 With gladness and with pain
I listen and make answer
 To the speaking waves again.

O River, bid me welcome!
   I have journeyed far and long
Since first I saw thy sparkle,
   And heard thy daybreak song;

And they are gone who sported
   Beside thy rose-rimmed shore ;
My heart returns to meet them,
   But they answer me no more.

The bravest and the gentlest
   Sleep near thy lulling wave;
And one, — thy waters call him far,
   But cannot find his grave.

Ah, that he too might slumber
   Under flag and flowery tree,
Where thy low perpetual measure
   Should bear him company!

Oh, tell me, rushing current,
   When the evening wind is low,
Do the voices of those lost ones
   Around thee come and go?

Thou givest me no answer;
　My question does thee wrong,
The joy of the Forever
　Is the burden of thy song.

Thou stayest not for losses,
　Thou hast no part with woe;
Thy theme is of To-morrow,
　And not of Long Ago.

There is no lamentation
　In Nature's faithful breast;
The leaves that fall beside thee
　She covers up to rest;

The lives that fall and wither
　She holds as close and dear,
Yet bids thee flow as brightly
　As if they still were here.

I would not bid thee linger
　To grieve o'er voices gone;
Into the further sunlight
　I, too, would follow on.

A WATER–LILY.

THOU nymph of woodland waters,
   White Naiad of the lake!
No flower of field or forest
   Thy beauty's crown may take.
Thy creamy petals glisten
   With glamours manifold;
A magic and a witchery
   Are in thy heart of gold.

With cheek upon the ripple,
   As pure as falling snow,
Thou wooedst me to linger;
   I could not let thee go.
And when thy lip of fragrance
   So softly touched my own,
I felt a recognition
   Even to my heart had flown.

Thus did Undine the peerless,
 In wonder-tale of old,
Uprising from the billow,
 Her destiny behold.
No more in soulless joyance
 To dance beneath the tide,
A human heart had sought her, —
 She looked, and loved, and died!

And now, the cool oar dripping,
 The ripple's broken song,
The bird that in the alders
 Was chirping low and long,
The glitter of the sunshine,
 The sky's entrancing blue,
One perfect day of summer
 From dawn to twilight dew, —

All these I press, together
 With this transcendent flower,
Within the book of poems
 Which cheers my lonely hour;
The minstrel and his verses
 The sweeter for thy sake,
O poet of the waters,
 White Naiad of the lake!

SUMMER'S PROMISE.

" NOW are the happy days of summer come!"
    Shouts the glad child; "now on the grassy lea
  I 'll chase the humming-bird and golden bee,
And hunt the Rainbow in her secret home."
Youth says: "It will be happiness to roam
  On the wide hills and by the gleaming sea;
  Hasten, O rosy days, and crown for me
Life's goblet high with pleasure's fairy foam!"
The summer brings a promise all her own
  To each and all; even he whose days are long,
  Of world-work weary, and from whom the fair
Illusion, Pleasure, is forever flown,
Looks upward when he hears the year's new song,
  And answers, "It is always summer *there!*"

THE TWO LIGHTS.

WITH a bold and brilliant lustre
From the isle across the bay
The lamp in the lighthouse turret
Sends forth its evening ray.
As over the waters that roll between
Falls its burnished pathway of golden sheen,
How pale in the distance, how dim and far,
Shines the evening star!

So the joy of the living present,
The human and palpable bliss,
Outdazzles the heaven above us,
So near and so precious is this.
While there's warmth for the heart and delight for the
eye,
We heed not the glory that bends from the sky;
Yet over us, patient and changeless and far,
Shines eternity's star!

THE FOREST BROOK.

DEEP in the greenwood a brooklet wanders
　　Under the quivering alder-leaves,
Through glimmering tree-tops a mellow lustre,
　　A veil of silver, the sunlight weaves.

Home of the twilight, mystical, moody,
　　Flutter of bird-wings, whisper of boughs,
Ever with pleading and fond entreaty
　　The brooklet murmurs as on it flows.

Dark-blue violets love to open
　　Their dusky eyes in this fairy glen,
Listen awhile to the singing ripples,
　　Droop in the gloaming and dream again.

Never weary of sweet communing,
　Brook and violets here are met;
Pure and fair in their summer wooing,
　Who that listens can e'er forget?

Oh, how peaceful this rare seclusion!
　Hither with yearning steps I come;
Rivulet, singing my childhood's story,
　Flowers of the forest, ye call me home!

A MESSAGE.

O ISLAND of Bermuda,
  Rose-garden of the deep!
Your brightest bloom and verdure
  For one dear stranger keep.
Of our rude winters weary,
  She seeks your kinder air;
Let the pure wine of summer suns
  For her be treasured there.

O coral-reefed Bermuda!
  When first upon your shore
She listens to the greeting
  Your white-robed billows pour,
Let not one stormy measure
  The peaceful music stir;
Bid all your ocean harpers wake
  Their gentlest tones for her.

O spice-winds of Bermuda!
  When at the close of day,
Amid the green palmettos
  You lightly toss and play,
If she should pause beneath them,
  Oh, bring your odors sweet,
Until the heart of summer-time
  Is lavished at her feet.

O roses of Bermuda!
  Wear now your richest dyes;
For she who bends above you
  Looks with a poet's eyes!
The answer to her rapture
  In words you cannot speak;
But give your warmest, ruddiest tints
  To live upon her cheek!

REST AND HEALING.

I.

REST, only rest! even if it be to sleep
   In long oblivion to be wholly blest;
      For life is a long weariness at best,
And into utter stillness I would creep.
Out of the whirl and clamor, in the deep
   And close embrace of Nature's mother-breast,
   Let pulseless hands to pulseless heart be pressed,
Forgetting how to labor or to weep.
Even my soul's self, uplifted from that bed,
   Though angels throng to meet and comfort me,
   Eager to know my dearest, first request,
Would say to them, "If time indeed is fled,
   And this be measureless eternity,
Let Heaven's first boon and blessedness be rest!"

II.

BUT this would pass, for even as I dream
   Of such Nirvâna as the utmost goal,
   My thoughts rebel against its long control,
And turn dismayed from Lethe's waveless stream.
Soon would the faces, hovering o'er me, seem
   Out of a rosy, luminous cloud to roll,
   And eyes of love would gaze into my soul,
Piercing its slumber with a living beam.
Not rest but joy will be the spirit's cure;
   The sunrise splendor of such happiness
   As lures me now in semblance and in sign;
Fresh will life's current flow, and swift and pure,
When hands of healing to my lips shall press
   The sacrament of that celestial wine.

A DREAM INTERPRETED.

I DREAMED my friend came back to me
   With the same look she wore of old, —
The soft brown hair, the beaming glance,
   Which I no more behold.

I thought I made my table bright
   With sparkling crystal, fruit, and flower,
As one makes haste to deck the board
   When nears the festal hour;

And while all stood expectant by
   And wondered who my guest would be,
I opened wide the outer door
   And called aloud on thee.

No sound came from the clouded sky,
  The night seemed empty as before;
But suddenly I saw thee stand
  Smiling within my door.

With eager words and lingering gaze
  I led thee to my outspread board;
My hands, that trembled with delight,
  The wine of welcome poured.

I woke; and at the window-pane
  I heard the wintry tempest moan.
Alas! it swept thy hillside grave
  Defenceless and alone.

Yet though the grave is dark and deep,
  And cold and high even heaven may be,
If only in my dreams, thou still
  Wilt come and sup with me.

Thy angelhood will oft again
  With me the wine of joy partake;
Thy pitying presence at my side
  The bread of sorrow break.

Death shuts and bars the door in vain,
   Faith flings the portal wide,
And shows the lost one smiling still
   Just on the other side.

THE RAINBOW.

BRIDGE of enchantment! for a moment hung
　　Between the tears of earth and smiles of heaven,
Surely the sheen of jasper, sapphire, gold,
　　Flashes and burns along thy colors seven,
　　　　And to the lifted heart, the beaming eye,
　　　　Reveals the splendor of the upper sky.

Whether as Northmen dream, the hero's soul
　　Enters its rest across thy brilliant height;
Or, as the more melodious Greek hath told,
　　Iris descends with message of delight;
　　　　Or in the silence beautiful is heard
　　　　The still, small whisper of the Hebrew Word;

Welcome forever to a stormy world,
　　Dear in each sign and symbol of the past
As of the future; for our Hope shall climb
　　Thy lustrous arch to realms unseen and vast;
　　　　Peace shall come down to us, and in thy light
　　　　God's finger still the golden Promise write!

THE FRIARS OF CASTINE.

MIDSUMMER'S prime is come at last, —
    The white-winged hour delayed so long,
With sunlight's sparkle on its plume,
    And ocean's murmur in its song;
It finds me musing o'er thy scene
Of storied beauty, fair Castine!

From this green rampart's velvet height
    The island village lies in view,
On every side a ribbon bright
    Encircling it, of ocean blue;
While seaward vanishes away
Against the sky the sparkling bay.

Who, looking on these tranquil isles
　Which drowsing in the sunshine lie, —
These ships like sea-birds on the wing
　Just hovering between sea and sky, —
Would dream this scene of summer charm
Had ever known the drum's alarm?

But not on battle's call nor charge
　My restful thought to-day would dwell;
On yonder field of sloping green
　Both friend and foeman slumber well.
The monks of old Acadian fame
This summer hush and reverie claim.

The saintly friars, — Capuchin, —
　Here found a place for work and prayer;
Amid the forest's silent gloom
　A chapel builded, rude and bare,
And to " Our Lady " sought to raise
In " Holy Hope " the chant of praise.

The New World held no glittering lure
　To win them from their native land;
To hermit life and rigorous toil
　They came, a self-devoted band, —
To bed of boughs, to scanty food,
And savage-haunted solitude.

At midnight rose their matin-hymn,
  With only startled birds to hear,
At morn and eve in silent prayer
  They sought the Virgin's pitying ear,
And brave and patient wrought to bless
The children of the wilderness.

Self-exiled from the sweet south land
  And all its favored clime had given,
Well pleased when with some sacred drops
  An Indian child was signed for heaven, —
Our simpler worship, purer creed,
May honor long such lofty deed.

The petals of the sunset rose
  Are falling fast upon the bay;
" Ave Maria " do I hear,
  Fainting and fading with the day?
Such echoes of the past, I ween,
Shall ever hallow old Castine.

THE VIGIL OF THE YEAR.

THE year has passed to its gloaming
    With a splendor of red and gold,
As if from the heavens a billow
    Of the sunset fire had rolled;

As if caught in the tremulous branches,
    And lost on the hills afar,
Were thousands of wandering sunbeams
    That had strayed from the gates ajar!

How deep is the hush of the woodlands!
    And over the meadows chill,
Where the summer song rang loudest,
    Now all is strangely still.

Is it that Nature calls us
    Her service of peace to share, —
After the song the silence,
    After the praise the prayer?

Answer, O restless spirit,
  And heart that is cold and sere,
To the wordless expectation
  That breathes from the passing year.

For far in the darkening forest
  The holly grows ripe and red,
And a new prophetic lustre
  On the sky of the east is shed.

Watch thou! for the hour is breaking
  When, with lips no longer dumb,
To the whisper, "The Christ is coming!"
  Thou shalt answer with song, "*He is come!*"

A SCARLET LEAF.

THIS scarlet bough which hangs above my door
    Is a perpetual picture of the woods,
And of a lake, with fringe of forest shore,
    Deep in their solitudes.

I see the silver ripples as they toss
    Against the long, unbroken line of green,
The red flame of the sumac thrown across
    The hillside's darker screen;

And where the breezy waters reach to lave
    The path that winds beneath a broken crag,
One scarlet maple hangs above the wave
    October's warning flag.

It was a place where Nature's self might lose
    All kinship with the restless human heart.
Yet even here I could not idly muse
    And unperceived depart;

For all the witching wood-nymphs were astir
 To bring their treasures to my passing gaze;
I heard swift, rushing feet in pine and fir,
 Soft wings amid the haze.

And thus the sylvan fays in silent glee
 Garnered the forest in my broken sheaf.
Woods, waves, and skies, — I keep them still with me
 Upon a scarlet leaf!

THE ANSWER.

THE people bore him with a strong appeal
    Unto the very altar of the Lord.
    Not two or three, — the world with one accord
Prayed that the Father would this once reveal
His healing power, and trust with blessing seal.
    "Let not," they cried, "this priceless blood be
        poured!
    This man so just, so mindful of thy word,
Go down to death, while nations for him kneel!"
Fame, Freedom, Love sighed, "Help this mortal
        strife!"
The Lord made answer, "*He indeed shall live.*"
Then lifted him among those orbs on high
Who have outlived the mystery of our life.
Ah! now we know though earth had much to give,
For him it was more glorious to die!

SUMMER'S SLEEP.

WHY this golden silence
  In the air and sky?
Listen! from the woodlands
  Lonely breezes sigh;
Through the empty branches,
  Long and low and deep
Murmurs Nature's slumber song, —
  Summer lies asleep.

On her sun-bright tresses
  Withered roses lie;
Sea and shore responsive
  Sound her lullaby.
Drowsy little rivulets
  Nestle out of sight;
Summer sleeps, and all the world
  Feels the hush of night.

Watched by sombre shadows,
  Wrapt in fleecy snow,
Nothing of the storm-strife
  Shall the dreamer know.
Though from midnight steeple
  Calls the Christmas bell,
Joy nor woe shall waken her;
  She will slumber well.

But at last a clamor,
  Musical and clear,
In the April daybreak
  Will salute her ear.
Only love's sweet accents
  Can her slumber break;
To her own dear birds and flowers
  Summer will awake.

COUNSEL.

"LOOK up, — not down!" The mists that chill and
    blind thee,
  Strive with pale wings to take a sunward flight;
Upward the green boughs reach; the face of Nature,
  Watchful and glad, is lifted to the light.
The strength that saves comes never from the ground,
But from the mountain-tops that shine around.

"Look forward, — and not back!" Each lost endeavor
  May be a step upon thy chosen path;
All that the past withheld, in larger measure,
  Somewhere in willing trust the future hath.
Near and more near the Ideal stoops to meet
The steadfast coming of unfaltering feet.

THE WOODS OF MAINE.

TO all the wide, wild woods of Maine
    The singing birds have come again;
In thicket dense and skyward bough
Their nests of love are builded now;
And daybreak hears one blithesome strain
From all the wide, wild woods of Maine.

In all the deep, green woods of Maine
The myriad wild-flowers wake again;
On mossy knoll, by whispering rill,
Their new life opens, shy and still;
Unseen, unknown, as spring days wane,
They sweeten all the woods of Maine.

The fair and fragrant woods of Maine!
To dwellers far on shore and plain

The forest's breath of healing flows
In every wandering wind that blows;
And life throbs fresh in every vein,
When bloom the boundless woods of Maine.

———

Now far from those sweet woods of Maine,
The song comes back, a sad refrain!
These pines and palms that speak no word
Of scenes that once my heart have stirred,
This cypress shade, these ivy bowers,
And long, unceasing march of flowers,

Are like an echo, faint and drear,
Of music I have ceased to hear.
Oh, while your choiring boughs you dress
In spring or autumn loveliness,
The green and gold you wear in vain
For one who loved you, woods of Maine!

UNDER THE PALM-TREE.

THE NEW ITALY.

A HUNDRED days of perfect summer sun,
  And yet the reign of splendor is not done!
A hundred days, each like a living flower
Whose amber bud unfurls at daybreak's hour,
Blossoms at mid-day in resplendent white,
And falls as falls the dying rose at night.

Serene and smiling land!
Watched by the mountains that around thee stand,
Rocked on the calm Pacific's sheltering breast,
Beneath the golden curtains of the west,
All that kind Nature gave that elder clime,
Her sun-child Italy,
She gives anew to thee.
All that once made that summer-land sublime
Thine own may be.

The skies of lustrous blue,
Heaven's color shining through,
The vineyards purpling wide
Valley and mountain-side,
The fig-tree's shade, the dusky cypress screen,
The almond's flag of white,
The palm's broad tent of coolness and delight,
The olive's glossy sheen,
The golden orange in its bower of green,
The soft and healing airs of Italy,
Nature bestows on thee.

And more, Italia's wealth of bloom,
Each precious, storied flower
With Eden's heritage of sweet perfume
Is of thy later dower.
The spicy Eucalyptus fills the air
With balsam strong and rare;
The graceful pepper and the laurel-tree,
And ivy wreathing all most royally,
Make beautiful the year.
Thy seasons know no death, for here
Time no decay nor desolation knows, —
His crown a fadeless rose.

In that rich hour when day and night keep tryst,
Lingering as lovers in the purple mist,
When in a sudden ecstasy expand
The thousand odors of this fragrant land,
Who that has lived amid its rare delight,
But feels his spirit quicken with the sight
Prophetic, of the glories to be wrought
When Art to Nature has her offering brought?

O Summer Queen! Thy Rome that is to be,
On her proud hills beside the sunset sea
Watches the hour of fate,
When Art, a pilgrim from her first estate,
Shall enter triumphing the Golden Gate!
When through thy farthest land,
Where now the crumbling earthen walls alone
Tell of the century flown,
Strong palaces and towers of fame shall stand,
With soaring shaft, and statue chastely wrought,
Each like a speaking thought,
A picture-language known
World wide and all thine own.

Let not the sculptor rear
The dead gods of the elder nations here.
Our own dawn-heroes wait

The touch of inspiration.   Lo! afar
There burned for ages a mysterious star,
A watch-fire on a mountain.   Long and late
A priestly line for untold centuries kept
That fire unquenched; for one whom they adored,
The sun-god of the Orient, who had poured
His mercy and his splendor on the land,
Had vanished, ages-wept,
Yet promised to return.   That fire no more
Sparkles upon the New World's midnight shore.
Gone is the priestly band —
He comes not yet.   Oh, let the sculptor take
That form sublime !   Let Quetzalcoatl wake
In deathless marble, and the gods who long
Inspired the Redman's song
Find thus their second coming, risen anew
In Art's divinest hue !

The Hindu deems that in each human breast,
At birth, a lotus-bud is closely pressed.
If evil rules and blights the growing years,
The leaflet, scentless, shrunken, disappears;
But let high thoughts and lofty deeds have sway,
And swell the lovely petals day by day,
Till in the prime of life, a priceless dower,
It floods the spirit with its radiant flower.

Youngest and fairest nursling of the West,
The lotus-bud is hidden in thy breast.
In rapt expectancy above thee bend
Nature thy mother, Art thy gracious friend.
Let dreams of glory now thy slumber stir,
Let Genius be thy dreams' interpreter;
So shall the lotus-soul within thee furled,
Blossom and brighten a rejoicing world.

LOS ANGELES.

" Nuestra Señora Reina de los Angeles."

SHE sits amid her orange-trees,
  Our Lady of Los Angeles,
   The smiling city of the sun,
And counts the seasons as they flee,
Like beads from off a rosary
   That slip and sparkle one by one.

Upon the outer solitudes
The demon of the desert broods,
   The ocean chafes and murmurs near;
But safe within her garden wall
She hears these ancient foemen call,
   With tranquil, inattentive ear.

At close of day from yonder height
I saw her robed in evening light,
   One white star like an opal showing;
Her roses drooped in slumber sweet,
But oh, the lilies at her feet
   Upheld their censers overflowing.

" Tell me," I said, " O city fair,
What dreams pervade this sunset air,
   What memories stir this purple splendor?
For surely magic worketh here,
And in the stillness I can hear
   Reverberations wild yet tender."

Was it enchantment? Suddenly all her roses had
   vanished !
Fled were the vestal lilies, their incense spilled and
   forsaken,
Palace and cottage were gone, and the orange-groves
   and the vineyards
Rolled away like a wave and were lost in the ocean of
   sunset.
It was the twilight age, when gods from the heaven
   descending,

Choosing some grassy dell or cañon bordered with pine-
    trees,
Made them lodges of boughs and dwelt among men and
    were happy.
But one unknown to them all had chosen this for her
    dwelling;
Perhaps she had wandered away from the land of frost
    and of glacier,
Or come from the cold sea-deeps, for her face was white,
    and speechless
She glided over the vale with a graceful, willowy
    motion.
Her robe was of silvery texture with woven pearls for
    her girdle,
Her tresses white as snow, a veil of ineffable splendor,
And all who looked in her face reflected its luminous
    beauty.
By day she dwelt unseen, but night after night she
    wandered
Pacing soft and slow the dewy emerald verdure,
And if some child awoke and cried out in midnight
    terror,
Lo! she stood in the door of his lodge and her sweet
    look calmed him.
Fain would the children of men have kept her always
    among them,

But a god, more mighty than they, with covetous eyes
    looked on her;
One who had dwelt with them long, — so long he had
    almost forgotten
His tent in the starry plains and the hunting-grounds of
    the morning, —
Followed her night by night and urged her to hear his
    devotion.
" High over hill and cloud," he said, " let us journey
    together;
I will build thee a lodge afar in the purple meadows,
With curtains of fleecy mist, and when thou shalt walk
    at even,
The stars at thy feet shall blossom, a garden of golden
    daisies."
Ah! though her face was cold, and her beautiful lips
    were silent,
The heart within her was warm and at last to his pas-
    sion responded.
Then came a night when in vain the children of men
    watched her coming, —
Hushed were the fragrant winds, and everywhere silent,
    trembling,
Old and young looked forth and waited in strange
    expectation.
Suddenly, up in the sky, forever away and above them,

Shone the beautiful face enveloped in snow-white
    tresses,
And they knew that the god who loved her had taken
    her up into heaven!
Age after age they bowed before her in fond adora-
    tion;
For though she was now the Moon, and queen of the
    heavenly gardens,
Once she had dwelt among them, dwelt in Los Angeles
    valley.

O Lady of Los Angeles!
Not on such eerie tales as these
    Let now thy musing fancy feed;
Though surely never moonlight fell
With such a wild enchanting spell
    On mount or glen or velvet mead.

It was thy happier fate to see
The Indians' rude idolatry
    Of spirits both of earth and heaven,
Of voices in the darkness heard,
Of serpent, beast, and singing-bird,
    From every ancient fastness driven.

What loftier music fills the ear?
What forms are these, approaching near,
  Their brows alight with coming day?
While up the shadowy mountain-side
The sullen tribes of darkness glide,
  And from the daybreak hide away?

Again a twilight veil enshrouded the dreamland valley,

Again the walls and spires and blossoming orchards
  vanished;

Wide spread the silent plain, and like the slow path of a
  serpent

Wound over glistening sands the trail of Los Angeles
  river.

Silent all, did I say? There is music heard in the
  distance!

Nearer it swells and nearer, a clangor of gladness and
  triumph.

And now, distinct to the vision, approaches a strange
  procession.

First come gray-haired men, the soldiers of many battles,

Loyal sons of Spain, grown old in her honored
  service;

After them walk the Fathers, priests of San Gabriel
  Mission,

9

Their Indian neophytes bearing the candles, the cross,
and the banner
On which like a holy lily is painted the face of Our
Lady.
Women were there and children, all lifting up jubilant
voices,
For here henceforth was their home, the royal gift of
their monarch.
Home! the word on their lips was sweet as the dew of
heaven!
Wayworn soldiers' wives, who had wandered and wept
full sorely
Since on the hills of Spain their dark eyes lingered in
parting.
And oh! the joy of the little ones, flitting from hands
that led them,
Greeting each startled bird and every flower of the way-
side
With ripples of happy laughter, enhancing the song of
gladness.
On they come, their hearts thrilled high with a fond
expectation, —
Visions of happy rest after long years of service,
Visions of rose-bowered cots in a land of perpetual
summer,
Olives and figs and grapes in gardens easily nurtured;

For their days of toil were over, and rest was their
    utmost longing, —

Rest, and the grateful worship of Mary, Queen of the
    Angels.

Thus the pioneers came into Los Angeles valley;

Hands clasped hands in joy where now is the shaded
    Plaza,

And while with ringing voices they chanted the loud
    Te Deum

And christened with musical name the home of their
    hope and longing,

San Bernardino looked down from his kingly throne in
    the distance,

And the Sierra Madre hills, with bare, brown fore-
    heads,

Stood in the breathless sunshine and *Benedicite* echoed.

    O city of Los Angeles!

    Thy days go on, — the days of peace;

      And wide along the fertile mead,

    Each in its garden Paradise,

    I see the Spanish dwellings rise,

      With earthen wall and roof of reed.

From every cottage sounds afar,
At setting of the morning star,
   The sunrise song.   A single voice
The strain begins; some aged dame,
Long waking, sees the brightening flame,
   And gives the signal to rejoice.

The old, the young take up the strain,
Till over all the dewy plain
   The hymn to the Madonna swells;
The priests glide noiseless o'er the sward,
And " Hail ! O Mother of the Lord ! "
   Clang out the shrill, exultant bells.

But this has ceased to be, and now,
Queen city, lift thy dreaming brow,
   Look onward, outward into time !
The sunrise song is of the past, —
What mightier music shall at last
   Be worthy of thy peerless clime?

I see thee like a vast white rose
Expand, until the desert glows
   A tawny captive at thy feet !
I see thy sunburnt mountains shine
With palaces, and at thy shrine
   Of Summer all the nations meet.

Smile on amid thy orange-trees,
O city of Los Angeles!
    Yet in thy coming hour of prime
Keep thou thy ancient legends dear,
And through all loftier pæans hear
    The echo of the Mission chime!

WINTER ROSES.

BENEATH an opalescent sky,
   A brilliant, boundless canopy,
  I walk the level street
  With lingering, aimless feet;

For now a garden tempts me on,
With heliotrope and ivy grown;
  Now from a sunny wall
  Resplendent lilies call;

Yonder a palm whose lofty grace
Breathes majesty of ancient race, —
  I hasten on to see
  The Old World's royal tree.

And in the luminous atmosphere
The velvet hills look warm and near;
   Their peaks of green and brown
   The garden-city crown.

Still on, regardless of the way,
Till under cypress-boughs I stray
   And find a green retreat,
   With banks of roses sweet.

How proud and beautiful they stand,
Insignia of the summer-land,
   The trophies she has won
   From the adoring sun!

Wet by the fountain's showery dews
Each blossom glows with peerless hues:
   Here the white rose lifts up
   Her pearly, humid cup;

And here are creamy buds that hold
An inner wealth of orient gold,
   And the vermilion-dyed,
   Superb in flowery pride.

And see ! pink-petalled like the morn,
The fairest rose of blossoms born
    Unfurls from mossy green
    Her orb of silken sheen.

Oh, this indeed is fairy ground !
Can dearer loveliness be found
    Than summer roses set
    In winter's coronet?

Ah, yes ! let all this rich perfume,
This opulence of tropic bloom
    Vanish, and give me back
    One gladness that I lack, —

The eyes where love's blue violet blows,
The cheeks that flush with love's own rose !
    My darling's smile would be
    All summer-land to me.

MOUNT HAMILTON.

WATCH-TOWER of the Pacific! As the mist
      And foam of daybreak down the valley glide,
Or surging high in waves of amethyst
   Flow back before the day's incoming tide,
Serene thou standest in the morning red,
Greeting the sunrise with uncovered head.

As roll the mists away, where now a sea
   Of vapor tossed, in many a rock-heaved crest
The billowy mountains lie. Thou seem'st to be
   A light-house, lifted from some ocean's breast,—
An ocean motionless and dumb and deep,
Smitten, in some dead past, with endless sleep.

Beyond these wave-like hills, in dreamy calm
   The vale of summer lies. A rich expanse
Of orchard, vineyard, gardens green with palm
   And flushed with roses, meet the eager glance.
There life is warm and new; the mission-bell
Alone repeats a century's song and knell.

The white Sierras like an armèd band
   Guard in long ranks the eastern gate of day;
Northward Diablo from his fortress grand
   Watches the golden city of the Bay;
Westward a single dazzling line of white
Shows where the blue Pacific meets the sight.

But not for this shall wise men from the East
   Ascend the winding path to Hamilton;
Fair as the view on which their eyes may feast,
   Sublimer scenes unfold at set of sun.
Earth yields her beauty to the morning light,
But heaven itself is opened to the night.

In hushed expectancy a noble guard
   Of mountains fitly named attendant waits;
Kepler, who heeded not the world's reward,
   Gazing, entranced, through wisdom's fairer gates,
Copernicus, who seized heaven's outer key,
Sad Galileo, ancient Ptolemy, —

These and their kindred searchers of the sky
   Wait the new revelations.   Unto them
Was given the scorn and scourge of bigotry;
   Not then as now the ready diadem
Of the world's praise and recompense to each
Interpreter of the celestial speech.

To the keen watchers on this mountain height
  God's writing on the skies shall be unrolled;
Star after star with lips of fire shall speak
  The secrets hid in hieroglyphs of gold;
The Moon shall draw aside her silver veil,
And even the Sun with angry wonder pale.

Oh, who can tell how soon the hour will be,
  When some large planet, drifting full in sight,
Shall send response across the ether sea
  To lightning-signal from this glorious height, —
When world to world shall answer from afar,
And life to come be promised by a star?

Calm be his rest who gave this lofty dome,
  Asking a grave beneath its corner-stone, —
A mausoleum which in time to come
  Shall be at once an altar and a throne.
For Science here as king, and Truth as priest,
Shall bid the world to a perpetual feast.

VESPERS IN SAN JUAN.

RING, bell from Spain, high in the mission tower,
   Ring out the sunset hour!
After the dry, brown day of dust and heat,
   Thy even-song is sweet.

The languid village hears the tuneful peal,
   And black-eyed women steal
Forth from their low-walled dwellings, one by one,
   Glad that the day is done.

Across the plaza come the sunburnt men,
   At home from toil again;
And beautiful, dark children run to play
   Along the cypress way.

With scent of ocean comes the evening gale
   Down San Benito's vale;
Through purpling vines and olives rustling low
   Its spicy footsteps go.

Around the church, through the long colonnade,
　Crumbling with age and shade,
Through the choir window, open to the night,
　Flutters the restless sprite,

Nor stays till it has found beyond the nave
　An altar-guarded grave,
And to the dead priest, waiting for the light,
　Whispered a hushed " good-night ! "

Ring, bell from Spain, high in the mission tower,
　Ring for the vesper hour !
Beyond the village, far along the plain,
　Bear on the melting strain.

The shepherd strolling listless and alone
　Hears the familiar tone,
And all unnoticed up the brown hill creep
　His cloud-like flock of sheep.

For now he seems to see Juanita's face,
　Fair through its veil of lace ;
Softly she glides within the mission door,
　Kneels on the earthen floor,

And while the altar candles faintly glow,
    And music ripples low,
She clasps her rosary in the stillness dim
    And breathes a prayer for him!

Oh what heeds he, drunk with the sunset balm
    Wafted from vine and palm,
That hands of holy zeal and hearts of prayer
    First made this valley fair?

And what to him that in the altar's shade
    Forever silent laid,
Sleeps he who first rung out that vesper bell
    And loved its music well?

He only sees the future's beaming cup
    To his warm lips held up, —
Juanita, and the cot that is to be
    Beneath his own fig-tree!

Ring, bell from Spain! From the dark mission tower
    Fast fades the sunset hour.
Sleep on, O priest, though bells peal high with joy!
    Be happy, shepherd boy!

AD ASTRA.

HARK! to the Voice which cries
　　To the valiant and the young, —
There is a measure sweeter far
　　Than any the Past has sung.

There is a deathless joy
For the true and loyal heart,
There are deeds no hero yet hath dared;
　　Gird thy sword on and depart!

Out of these cloister days
Into the wide world go;
Out of the gray night of the Past,
　　Enter the sunrise glow!

There is a language of fire
To fall on lips that are dumb,
And to him who is nearest the inner shrine
Shall the blissful utterance come.

Fruit of ambrosia grows
On the mountain's sunward side;
But only for him who with feasts of earth
Is still unsatisfied.

There is a path which leads
Through the lowly and the real
To highlands beautiful and far, —
The soul's supreme ideal.

Those heights are only won
By the strongest of the strong;
Follow that path and make thine own
Banner and crown and song.

A ROSE OF JERICHO.

"WHY do you take my garden rose,
　　Still fresh and glowing, from the vase,
And give a dry and withered stalk
　　My favorite's dewy place?"

"Lady," he said, "there came a day
　　When far across the burning plain
Slow crept, as hour by hour went by,
　　A winding camel-train.

"And none in all that wandering band
　　Who sought with me the Orient's shrine,
Concealed beneath the pilgrim's garb
　　So sad a heart as mine.

"But while with mournful thoughts I mused,
　　Light blown, as if from fairy bower,
Came fluttering o'er the yellow sand
　　To me this magic flower.

"I knew its folded petals hid
　　The breath and bloom of other days,
And that some happier hour might give
　　Its beauty to my gaze.

"Through all the paths of Palestine,
　　And wide across the stormy sea,
My cherished rose of Jericho
　　I brought to home and thee.

"And now the secret of my soul
　　I to the wizard rose have told,
And if to-morrow's light shall see
　　Its dusty scroll unrolled,

"If life and bloom and odor come
　　Again as from a grave set free,
The rose of Jericho will tell
　　That secret wish to thee!"

The morning beams; the lady steps
  Expectant to her garden bower;
Behold! the withered stem upholds
  A rare, mysterious flower!

A subtle odor steals abroad;
  The petals gleam with golden hue;
It is as if the wanderer's heart
  Had opened to her view.

A step draws near; there is no need
  For words to tell what roses know;
To utter love's own speech has flowered
  The rose of Jericho.

THE KINGDOM OF THE CHILD.

OUT of the common daylight of the world
      I wandered forth into a golden dawn,
A buoyant and a brilliant atmosphere,
In which all language had a sweeter sound,
All faces shone, and salutations glad,
Of love and cheer, flew fast from lip to lip.
Then as the light grew strong upon the heights,
Bell answered bell with jubilant refrain,
Until the hills the flying echoes caught
And wafted upward even to heaven itself.
And then there was a silence and great peace,
While in the air around me and above
A whisper rose that grew into a song, —
" Enter the happy kingdom of the Child! "

Oh then a miracle befell my sight!
With eyes no longer holden I beheld

A realm immeasurable, a golden zone
That like a ring of flame shone round the world.
And everywhere the joy was in the air,
Wreaths bloomed in every window, and so sweet
The incense rose from every heart and home,
It seemed a bright new world within the old.
And still the burden of a song went on,
Too silver-sweet for any human voice, —
" This day began the kingdom of the Child ! "

" Oh, who," I cried, " is lord of this fair realm?
Why do all hearts leap up with victor's joy?
I see no lofty forts, no steel-clad ranks,
Nor signs of martial conquest.   Can he be
A warrior and a king of high renown
Whose wide dominions thus unguarded lie? "
The answer came: " By mightier force than arms
Our monarch has his royal honor proved.
His truth is keener than a thousand swords;
His purity so dazzling that the hosts
Of unclean error flee before the sight,
And in the fervid summer of his love
The superstitions of the elder world
Like vapors of the sunrise disappear.
Look now upon the train of vanquished kings
Who bow before the sceptre of the Child ! "

Then down the borders of this shining land
There passed a gloomy train, and by their front
Majestic, awful even in their fall,
I knew them not as warriors but as gods, —
Osiris, dear to Egypt's ancient shrines,
And Isis the world-mother at his side,
Whose single tear renewed the wasted Nile.
They too, the bright Olympian deities,
With echoes of remembered music still
Upon their lips, regretfully passed by;
And the stern monarchs of the icy North, —
Odin, a wanderer from the fallen throne
Of old Valhalla, and the hoary Thor,
No longer glorying in his strong right hand.
And as they passed, the wilderness gave up
Its tawny gods, the spirits of the storms,
The mountains and the precipices wild.
And all walked heavily with bended head,
Save only Isis, in whose mourning eyes
I saw a wistful yearning for the Child.

As these strange shadows of the fallen faiths
Slowly departed, over all the sky
A soft, serene illumination grew,
A rosy and ineffable morning light;

And forth from cot and bower and palace came
Myriads of little children, bounding forth
With lilies-of-the-valley in their hands,
And fragrant boughs of forest evergreen.
These went before, and with them followed on
An army with white banners borne aloft,
On which in shining letters was inscribed
The legend beautiful, " Good-will to men."
" These are his guards and warriors," said the voice;
" See how the wayside blooms beneath their feet."
Then I, in haste of sudden ecstasy,
Said to the viewless spirit at my side,
" If eyes can bear such splendor, let me look
Upon the face of him you call the Child ! "

Then like a cloud the pageant disappeared,
And a pale orient landscape was unveiled, —
Wide plains in moonlight splendor, olive-boughs
Rocking beneath the nests of wakeful birds,
And, lighted by one radiant morning star,
The straw-thatched stable of a humble inn.
There in a manger, warm with breath of kine,
Behold ! the mystery of all mysteries,
The joy in sorrow and the light in gloom,
Heaven in earth's lowliness, God in the Child !

No crown he wore, but round his peaceful brow
An aureole shone, from whence unnumbered rays
Floated away to crown less worthy heads.
His hand no sceptre clasped, but fast and far
The beams of morning as his heralds rode
To bear the Christmas gladness to the world;
And fast and far his dearer angels sped,
Blessing the little children and the poor
With the best utterance of his perfect love.
And sorrow heard, and grieving lips were still,
And evil hid itself and was afraid.
Oh, then with heart at rest I heard again
The voice that swelled and grew into a song, —
"This day, till time shall end, from shore to shore
Shall come the blessed kingdom of the Child!"

THE ANGELUS.

RING soft across the dying day,
  Angelus !
Across the amber-tinted bay,
The meadow flushed with sunset ray,
Ring out and float and melt away,
  Angelus.

The day of toil seems long ago,
  Angelus !
While through the deepening vesper glow,
Far up where holy lilies blow,
Thy beckoning bell-notes rise and flow,
  Angelus.

Through dazzling curtains of the west,
  Angelus,
We see a shrine in roses dressed,

And lifted high, in vision blest,
Our every heart-throb is confessed,
    Angelus!

Oh, has an angel touched the bell,
    Angelus?
For now upon its parting swell
All sorrow seems to sing *Farewell;*
There falls a peace no words can tell,
    Angelus!

THE PALACE BUILDER.

JULIAN, a youth of fortune and of birth,
　　Whose hands the Fates had filled
With choicest gifts of earth,
And all his wishes royally fulfilled,
Lived for the Beautiful alone; he gave
To Art his days as worshipper and slave.
For this in wild and woodland paths whate'er
In Nature's realm was delicate and rare
With sensitive eye he sought, and every hue
Of billowy mead or mountain forest knew;
Then with swift touches on the canvas laid
Warm waves of light or cooler depths of shade.
Gems too of poesy he tireless sought,
And fed upon their sweetness in his thought.
Thus all his days in solitude were spent,
With what his wealth and taste had given, content.

Not even the pride of Art he worthy deemed
Of wider effort; yet he once had dreamed,
In early fantasies,
Of building a vast palace.   Grand and fair
He dreamed its golden towers should pierce the skies;
Its gardens should be rich beyond compare;
And in a marble court, enshrined in flowers,
Music perpetual should entrance the hours.

One day he sat beneath his linden-trees,
Musing in thoughtful ease;
A rivulet tinkled softly at his feet,
And the birds, fearless of his well-known face,
Poised on the branches with alluring grace,
Fluttered, but sang not in the noonday heat.
While lost in pleasing reverie, suddenly
One stood beside him with a brow of flame,
Looked on him steadfastly and spoke his name.
He, conscious that a being from on high
Had spoken, could but falter, " Here am I ! "
" Where is the palace that thy heart decreed ? "
The angel said.   " Of beauty thou indeed
Hast garnered richly, yet long years have given
Superior boons for which thou hast not striven.
Now let thy life's achievement be revealed
Unto thine eyes unsealed."

Then waved the branches of the linden-trees
As if swept strongly by a sudden breeze,
And vanished; and a garden met his eyes,
Dazzling his senses with its rich surprise.
Awhile he wandered blithely up and down
The rosy terraces, but weary grown
He looked in vain for any place of rest.
Flowers, fountains, bright cascades and bowery trees,
Beautiful vines and verdure, — only these.
The angel heard unspoken his request
And stood beside him. "Wouldst thou know?" he said,
"What spell would bid enduring walls arise?
Behold! the indolent pleasure thou dost prize
Can but a momentary fragrance shed;
Nobler the deeds, with purer purpose wrought,
Which shall uprear the palace of thy thought."

The vision changed. While Julian startled heard
The warning voice, a sullen, distant roar,
The shout of the invader at the door
Of Fatherland, with instant passion stirred
His wakened soul. "If glory will upraise
My palace towers, then shall the echoing praise
Of thousands greet my name!" He roused a band
Of loyal followers; eagerly he sought
The field where deeds of fame were swiftest wrought

And soonest crowned.   The bright sword in his hand
With eager radiance flashed.   To win a name,
To wrest the plume and coronal of fame,
So burned within his breast, that like a flame
It shone upon his features, and led on
His comrades like the shout of battle won.

There came a day
Of fearful carnage.   Julian wounded lay
Upon the field, and from his followers far,
Saw night shut down.   Not even a friendly star
Beheld him creeping painfully to rest
His head upon a soldier's lifeless breast.
There while he sighed alone he saw once more
The Being Wonderful, and as before,
With face that shone with more than sunrise flame,
He looked, and spoke his name.

"Julian!   The garden of thy past delight
Now holds the proud walls of thy warrior life;
Look upward!"   Then in rosy waves the night
Was overflowed, a rolling tide of light,
And where had seemed but now the field of strife
Was the remembered garden.   Oh how fair
Glittered the palace that was builded there!

Then as before through all the place he sped,
From room to room, and up with flying tread
To the great tower from which a banner flung
Broad folds of crimson. Suddenly he stayed
His eager steps and listened. Far or near
No sound of living utterance met his ear,
Nor love nor joy in grateful accents rung.
Silence was over all. Chilled and dismayed
He turned to meet his guardian. "Not for this,"
He cried, "have I foregone my early bliss,
And given my life to win a lofty name.
In this mute splendor all my proud hopes fade,—
There is no joy nor recompense in fame."

Serene the angel answered,—"Yet once more
Thou must go forth and life's last lesson prove.
The melody of living flows from love.
Though thy heart's blood thou on its threshold pour,
Hollow and dumb the walls of Fame shall be,
Nor one true voice of comfort answer thee.
But hasten now; redeem thy selfish past;
To God and fellow-man be true at last!
Be camp or court or wilderness thy place,
Thy strength, thy genius as oblation give
For the uplifting of thy age and race.
God and thy fellow-man will make life sweet to live!"

"God and my fellow-man!" Aloud he spoke,
And with the words in deep amazement woke,
For lo! it was a dream. The rivulet played
As softly on, and in the deepening shade
The birds he knew their even-song essayed.
"A dream?" he cried, — "a vision 't is to me!
O soul of mine, no longer shalt thou be
Defrauded of thy rightful royalty!
For reverently I take
The message, and this vow responsive make, —
The palace Heaven has shown me shall be mine!
Gardens and pillared halls and singing shrine,
And on the gateway shall this legend shine, —
For love of man and faith in the Divine!"

PERSEPOLIS.

HERE is the royalty of ruin; nought
　　Of later pomp the desert stillness mars;
Alone these columns face the fiery sun,
Alone they watch beneath the midnight stars.

Forests have sprung to life in colder climes,
Grown stalwart, nourished many a savage brood,
Ripened to green age, fallen to decay,
Since this gray grove of marble voiceless stood.

Not voiceless once, when, like a rainbow woof
Veiling the azure of the Persian sky,
Curtains of crimson, violet, and gold
In folds of priceless texture hung on high!

And what have sun and shadow left to us?
What glorious picture in this marble frame,
Ever, as soundless centuries roll by,
Gives this lone mount its proudest, dearest fame?

The sculptured legend on yon polished cliff
Has lost its meaning.   Persia, gray and old,
Upon her bed of roses sleeps away
The ages, all her tales of triumph told.

But here Queen Esther stood; and still the world,
In vision rapt, beholds that peerless face,
When, with the smile which won a throne, she gave
Joy to her king and freedom to her race.

OUR WITNESSES.

BY the immortals who attend us here
  We know ourselves immortal; all our way
Is guarded night and day
By presences from a diviner sphere,
Who ever hear and heed
The heart's most hidden need,
And ready whisper their eternal cheer.

Who has beheld the countenance of Hope?
Who knoweth if her eyes
Are colored like the skies?
And when in shadow-land we darkly grope,
Though close she walks beside us, who has seen
Her garment's texture or her sandals' sheen?
When hath the rapt ear heard
One silver-spoken word?
Yet were the world forsaken but one day
By Hope, oh, who till set of sun could stay?

Who hath had speech with Dreams?
At their own will they come
When weary eyes are dull and lips are dumb,
And every slumbering sense unconscious seems;
They open with a magic key
The spirit's door, and set the prisoner free.
Oh, then with what winged feet,
Soundless and fleet,
We flit outside the boundaries of the night!
How into past and future we take flight,
And even pass the threshold still and white
Where they who loved us — oh, so long ago! —
Look in our eyes and bid us see and know!

By many names we call
The viewless ones who hold in happy thrall
Our clinging natures.   Theirs no passing breath;
They reign victorious over change and death,
And keep the old world young.
Beauty, that in the fading blooms of time
Gives hint and token of a fairer clime
Than ever eye hath seen or voice hath sung;
Love, in all depths of parting and of pain,
Uttering the promise, *We shall meet again;*
And Joy, though we may know her but a day,

Even as she vanishes looks back to say,
" Hither is happiness, — oh, come away ! "

Surely immortals wait
Upon immortals.   Not in vain do we
Read signals of a grander destiny,
And in our exile pine for kingly state.
The Seen is but the shadow; the Unseen
Is the true light, and, changeless and serene,
Cheers our approach to that mysterious goal
Called death, which is the daybreak of the soul.

THE ORIGIN OF BIRDS.

THE Indians of the Shasta Mountains tell
 A legend strange and beautiful. They say
That the Great Spirit stepped from cloud to cloud,
  In the primeval day,

And first upon the dome of Shasta stood,
 The spotless face of new-born earth to see,
And everywhere He touched the land, upsprang
  A green, luxuriant tree.

Pleased with the sight, the splendor of His smile
 Melted the snows and made the rivers run,
And soon the branches tossed their leafy plumes
  And blossomed in the sun.

Day after day while that first summer shone
 He watched with fresh delight the growing trees;
But autumn came, and fast the bright leaves fell,
  Swept by the keener breeze.

Yet were they radiant now, in every hue
  Of red and gold which could with sunset vie;
Looking on them He loved them, — they were still
    Too beautiful to die!

Thrilled by His quickening gaze, each leaf renewed
  Its life, and floated buoyantly along;
Its beauty put forth wings, and as it soared
    Its gladness grew to song.

Thus from the red-stained oak the robin came,
  The cardinal-bird the maple's splendors bore,
The yellow-bird the willow's faded gold
    In living plumage wore.

Even the pale-brown leaves the pageant joined,
  Sparrow and lark awakened to rejoice,
And though they were less fair, He gave to them
    The more melodious voice.

Since then the birds close kinship with the trees
  Have ever kept, and build the yearly nest
Beneath the fragrant shelter of the boughs,
    As on a mother's breast.

THE PEPPER-TREE.

SIT with me, love, beneath the pepper-tree, —
    The mid-day air is mild,
And sapphire skies smile bright response to thee,
    My blue-eyed summer child!
Just a soft whisper from the distant bay
Flutters the fern-like leaves that o'er us sway.

The tree is old.   A strange and silent life
    Its growing years have known;
No brook has been its playmate, no fair lake
    Its pictured beauty shown;
No river, lingering with a lover's song,
Woke the young boughs and lightly passed along.

It never saw the glory of the leaves
   In Autumn's royal train:
Itself unfading, in perpetual green
   It watched the rank, wild plain,
And shadeless, sunburnt hills, whose last wild flower
Withered before the summer's ripening hour.

Perhaps, while chimed afar the mission bell,
   Here Spanish lovers strolled,
And as they stood beneath the listening tree,
   The sunset's fairy gold
Rained through its branches, till their lifted eyes
In vision saw the bloom of Paradise.

Some brother in the grave Franciscan garb,
   Crossing the lonely plain,
Murmured a blessing on these cooling boughs
   Which whispered " Peace " again.
Oh, did his benediction guard the tree,
That it has lived to shelter thee and me?

Now, happy tree! it dwells no more alone;
   Our garden's crown and pride,
It sees a crowd of fresh young foliage climb
   Luxuriant at its side;
And humming-bird and gold-winged butterfly
Drain the sweet flowers that in its shadow lie.

Yonder the palm-tree lifts it feathered plume,
   The cypress builds its bower,
The oleander, tall and proud, uplifts
   Its coronal of flower,
And the dark, damask rose thou lovest best,
Clings nearest to the pepper's patriarch breast.

Sit with me, then, within the fragrant shade,
   My blue-eyed summer child;
Forget that far beyond the rolling hills
   A dearer home hath smiled.
While sun and bloom their strong wine pour for thee,
My world is here, beneath the pepper-tree.

CRADLE–LIFE.

IS not this world the cradle of the soul,
    In which we rock, through restless infancy,
To music of the spheres?   At times we weep,
And long for baubles just beyond our reach,
Restrained from our desires, yet comforted
By the great Love which holds us.   We rejoice
In pleasant sounds mysterious to the sense,
Not yet awake to Mother Nature's speech;
We love the blue, sun-painted draperies
About us, and the corridors of green,
And view with still delight the beautiful
Glad faces of the stars which smile above.
Comforted, chided, nourished, we abide,
And know not whence we come to this new life,
Nor whither we shall go.   But in the grave
We lay aside our robes of infancy;
Then do we grow in stature, we are strong,
We walk abroad, and live the life we dreamed.

HALCYON DAYS.

TO all true lives there comes a time
    When doubt and care and tumult cease,
And wide across the spirit rolls
    A wave of peace;

When rocked upon the tranquil tide,
We look with wondering glances back,
For lo! where darkness was, God's smile
    Illumes our track.

We see the sorrows of the past
As through a luminous halo beam,
The darkest griefs that we have known,
    Transfigured seem.

From the black gulf that tossed us long,
The perfect pearl of peace is cast,
On the bleak skies the rose of joy
    Unfurls at last.

And singing thoughts, like Halcyon birds,
Drift lightly o'er the waveless calm,
Near and more near the summer shore,
    The isles of balm.

Oh, clouds again this light may veil,
Yet can no more our pathway dim;
God's smile once seen, we press straight on
    To Heaven and Him.

MOUNTAIN FLOWERS.

THESE wild flowers from the hills have filled my
    room
With strange magnificence. Amid their bloom,
    An unfamiliar guest,
I stand amazed; such high, imperial air,
Such pomp of color these bright blossoms wear, —
    Proud strangers of the West!

How beautiful they are! Celestial blue
The harebells lift their delicate sprays to view,
    And warm with golden rays
The poppies hold their satin splendors up,
And the wild daisy in its gilded cup
    A gem of dew displays.

These lilies, white, but dashed with crimson fires,
Are daughters of the sun.   These purple spires
   Grew on a crag so high,
The robes of morning and of evening swept
Their opening buds, and their ripe petals kept
   The kisses of the sky.

And yet, as one entranced may stand alone
In some great festival where all unknown
   A thousand faces glow,
And suddenly from far, forgotten days
Some shadow-face, with pleading, tender gaze,
   Revives the Long Ago, —

So as I gaze upon these haughty flowers
Of the Sierras, dear New England bowers
   Breathe back their lost perfume;
I see the mayflower with its flush of pink,
And sweeter still upon the river's brink
   My own wild roses bloom.

THE SISTINE MADONNA.

I.

BEHOLD, as in vision sublime,
  The flower of the fulness of time!
The type of all loveliness human,
The one ever-glorified woman!
  An angel, a goddess she seems,
As borne on the violet air,
Self-poised and transcendently fair,
A high, starry presence she beams.
  Yet those beautiful, sibylline eyes
Have wept as no goddess could weep;
And angels have leaned from the skies
To look on her blessedness deep,
  When on sorrow's eternal release,
  Fell the sunlight of infinite peace.

Though ever would Raphael paint
The Virgin, the Mother, the Saint,
Though his pencil was dipped in the fire
Of a ceaseless, adoring desire,
Once only the true Mary came!
O woman majestic and mild,
Our Lady of holiest fame!
Let me muse on thy beauty, and be
Uplifted, transported with thee,
In the smile of the long-promised Child!

II.

O poet-mother! first to sing
Earth's welcome to the coming King,
A thousand lips, since thine, have striven
To catch the echoed notes of heaven,
But thy *Magnificat* alone
Rings down the ages; still unknown
To living singer, the strong fire,
The joy superb, the pure desire
Which rung from thy exultant lyre.

The Orient skies were bright afar
With beams of Bethlehem's dawning star,

And Song herself, for thy sweet sake,
To noblest utterance was awake.
The long lament of seer and priest,
The sigh of waiting centuries ceased,
When from those loving lips was poured
Of victory's song the first, rich chord, —
  " My soul doth magnify the Lord ! "

III.

How beautiful the days
  While He is all her own !
While the world goes its stormy ways
To Mother and to Child unknown.
His head is pillowed on her breast,
Her song at evening soothes His rest,
And ere His lips to language move,
His soft looks utter boundless love.
Ah ! much she ponders; shadows deep
Across her vision come and go.
Must these sweet eyes yet learn to weep?
Must Israel's king share Israel's woe?

At times with piercing gaze she sees
Fulfilled the Scriptures' dark decrees;

The wine-press yields its scarlet flood,
The cross reveals its awful sign,
And every flower of Palestine
Drops fiery dew of holy blood.
And what beyond?   O mother-eyes!
Ye rend the secret of the skies!
O mother-love! not heaven can hide
The sword which shall thy heart divide,
  Nor veil in rayless mystery
  The beautiful, the boundless sea
  Of blessedness that is to be!

With gentlest touch, with murmured word,
The Child her tenderer mood has stirred.
She clasps Him close, — her own is He,
Hereafter all the world's to be;
But oh, not yet!   Upon her breast
His head shall softly, surely rest, —
Still far the glory or the woe
Of coming years.   Enough to know
The Prince of Peace to earth is given,
And finds her love His childhood's heaven.

A BURMESE PARABLE.

WITH look of woe and garments rent,
　　She walked as one whose strength is spent,
And in her arms a burden dread
She bore, — an infant cold and dead.
Men stood aside and women wept,
As through the gathering throng she crept,
And fell at last, with covered face,
Before the Buddha's seat of grace.

With startled gaze each Brahmin priest
Drew near; at once the Master ceased
His golden words, for he could read
The suffering spirit's inmost need,
And give with subtlest skill the cure
Which best that spirit could endure.
He bade her speak. She faltered wild,
" They told me thou couldst heal my child !"

"It may be so, but thou must bring
To me this simple offering, —
Some seeds of mustard which have grown
By homes where death was never known,
Nor tears have fallen beside the grave
Of mother, brother, child, or slave.
Go to the happy and the free,
And of their store bring thou to me."

She rose in haste, and all that day
She went her melancholy way.
No door was shut, for pitying eyes
Her quest beheld in kind surprise;
But every stranger answering said,
"We too have looked upon the dead, —
We too have wept beside the grave
Of mother, brother, child, or slave."

At set of sun alone she stood
Within the vine-entangled wood,
And uttered sadly, " I perceive
That every living heart must grieve.
Brief happiness had made me blind
To common griefs of humankind;
My eyes are open now to see
That all the world has wept with me."

Beneath the branches sweet and wild
She made a cradle for her child,
And watched until she saw afar
The village lamps, star after star,
Gleam, burn, and fade. " Our lives," she said,
" Like lamps of night will soon be fled;
Sleep soft, my child, until I come
To share thy rest and find thy home."

BEAUTIFUL DREAMS.

SHE lay unconscious in heavy sleep
    While her life-tide was ebbing slowly;
We knew she would pass with the sinking sun,
    As we watched by her pillow lowly.
And vainly we waited the farewell word, —
One whisper only the silence stirred, —
    " Beautiful dreams! beautiful dreams!"

Again we listened, — she slumbered on;
    Like a leaf in the light wind shaken
Her breathing fluttered, her pulse beat low,
    We feared she would never waken.
Again she lifted her lustrous eyes,
And uttered aloud in glad surprise, —
    " Such beautiful, beautiful dreams!"

No more.　On the wings of those lovely dreams
　She was gone, and the day was ended;
As we folded her hands to their last repose,
　The evening shades descended,
And the stars came out and wrote on high
In golden letters the mystery, —
　"Beautiful dreams! beautiful dreams!"

Ah! no mere vision of other days,
　Of youth's remembered story,
Illumed her fair and fading face
　With so rapturous a glory.
Shining across death's coming night,
From the land that was breaking on her sight,
　Came those beautiful, beautiful dreams.

White hands beckoned across the flood,
　Sweet lips uttered, "Come over!"
Eyes looked a welcome that never shone
　In the gaze of mortal lover.
Lingering, listening, drifting away,
She could only smile upon us and say, —
　"Beautiful dreams! beautiful dreams!"

LOST.

TWO friends to my youth were given,
  When life wore the bloom of May,
And with ardent lips they promised
  To garland my autumn day.

But one, with her pale hands folded,
  And white flowers on her breast,
Sleeps well, and her children's kisses
  Still hallow her place of rest.

The other, — ah! life has changes
  Whose meaning we fail to see,
And she, in the world of pleasure,
  Is happy — away from me.

The one comes often at midnight,
And under the dreamland stars
Her face is aglow with a beauty
Which no earthly shadow mars.

And she tells me over and over
That her love is deathless now,
And the touch of her kiss electric,
As I waken, is on my brow.

From the other a white-winged message,
Tossed off in an idle hour,
Comes now and then to stir me
With the old love's lingering power.

Oh, say, — for I cannot utter
The name which I cherish most, —
Of the two who have loved and left me,
Which shall I mourn as lost, —

The friend whom long, sweet summers
Have blossomed and rained above,
But who still surrounds and upholds me
In the spell of her infinite love;

Or the living, the unforgotten,
  Who, borne on the sparkling, bright
World-tide of passion and pleasure
  Has drifted out of my sight?

O love in the starry spaces,
  Thou art not yet lost to me!
O friend on the tide of fortune,
  I sorrow alone for thee!

EVEN–SONG.

DEPART in peace, fair day!
   Go to the soundless shore;
Thy burden and thy brief delight
   Shall come to us no more.
As sinks thy last beam in the west,
   We sing thee into rest.

We need not watch nor fear
   The clouds above us rolled;
One, in whose tender care we trust,
   Doth every moment hold,
And of our morrows none shall be
   Let loose from destiny.

In Him we work or rest,
  God giveth while we sleep;
And in full time our inmost right
  And recompense we reap.
At last, if patient we abide,
  We shall be satisfied.

Then while the darkness falls
  Soft as a folded flower,
Let us hold closer to His hand,
  And lean upon His power.
By winding ways and steps unknown
  We come unto our own.

THE ROSE BY THE WAYSIDE.

IT is told in an Eastern story
   That when Mary took her flight
With the Holy Child to Egypt,
   Slow journeying on by night,

Wherever in wild or desert
   They paused for a brief hour's rest,
The place of their hasty slumber
   With a springing rose was blest.

In her was the love unspotted,
   And the life of the world in Him;
What wonder a power supernal
   Went out on the night air dim.

And the breeze bent low to bear it,
  Earth lifted her brooding breast,
And the flower of flowers most precious
  Embowered that sacred rest.

How often with happy meaning
  The story comes back to me,
When some trusting, humble pilgrim
  On the journey of life I see,

Who, walking a desert pathway
  From the joyous world afar,
Hears ever the Christ-child's whisper,
  Sees ever the love-lit star!

Who with word of cheer unfailing,
  And love's perpetual grace,
Gives a beautiful adorning
  To the solitary place.

Oh, fresh and sweet were the roses
  That pillowed Madonna's head,
But they blossom to-day wherever
  The pure and the faithful tread.

VICTORY.

VICTORY blossoms in every clime,
   A tree sublime,
Of colors rare as the rainbow dyes
   In midsummer skies.
For the soldier it tosses a crimson plume,
Of smoke and of battle its rank perfume;
   On his heart in the carnage dire
   It burns like a flower of fire.

It thrives in the groves of solitude
   For the scholar's mood,
Purple and scentless, a part of the shade,
   Yet it cannot fade.
For the poet it throbs like a golden star,
As bright with beams and alas! as far.
   And he waits as the years go by
   The bloom of eternity.

But for him who ever in deed and word
   Is for others stirred,
Who gives his heart's blood with sword or pen
   For his fellow-men,
Only for him does this blossom show
Fair as sunlight and white as snow.
   Life's most beautiful dower,
   Victory's perfect flower!

13

"ALL'S WELL."

HAIL! fellow-pilgrim, wherefore haste?
　　The night is falling, dark with storm;
My evening bread is sweet to taste,
　　The glow upon my hearth is warm.
　　　　Long is thy path and wild and lone, —
　　　　His eyes looked deep into my own, —
　　　　　　"All 's well!"

Thy robe is rent by brier and thorn,
　　Thine eyes have known the pain of tears;
And on thy patient brow are worn
　　Deep furrows that are not of years.
　　　　"My staff is broken, but my palm
　　　　Still keeps the morning's fragrant balm;
　　　　　　All 's well."

Thou art forsaken and alone;
　　Thou lookest back with wistful gaze.
Some dream of beauty, still unblown,
　　Has mocked thee all these weary days.

" Heaven took the flower of life, to give
A bloom which shall forever live.
All 's well ! "

And thou art wounded! From thy side
The life-drops fall. O pilgrim, stay !
Wait for the ebbing of the tide,
And for the breaking of the day.
"Comrades invisible to thee
Beckon and call and signal me
All 's well !

" Follow me not, nor seek to hold
My spirit from its true repose ;
The shelter of that flowery fold
Will heal all wounds of friends or foes.
I go from dark to light, from strife
To perfect peace, from death to life !
All 's well ! "

Yet answer once before we part,
Thy voice uplifts and makes me free, —
Whence is this gladness of the heart,
This undertone of victory?
"I dimly see ; I am but dust,
But through all darkness I can trust !
All 's well ! "

IN WHAT SOIL DOES COURAGE GROW?

IN what soil does courage grow?
  Where the sunbeams warmest shine?
  Where the flowers of fortune twine
And her scented breezes blow?

> *On the bleak and rugged height,*
> *In the chill and starless night,*
> *Courage struggles to the light.*

In what garden blossoms trust?
  Is it where the summer dew
  Lights up every dainty hue,
And the roses never rust?

> *Not till rending storms sweep by*
> *Does the spirit make reply*
> *To the Master's, " It is I ! "*

Tell me where is triumph found?
  Work is weary, victory far,
  Underneath what happy star
Is the laurel's native ground?

    Pomp and praise and gain are nought,
    Noblest fame is dearest bought
    Death must seal what life has wrought.

WHY?

"WHY?" is a question that earth cannot answer;
　　Ages on ages have asked it in vain.
"Thou who hast poured for us life's mingled portion,
　　Why must we quaff it in sorrow and pain?"

Why?　All is silent.　Then *how* shall we drink it?
　　Now in swift eloquence Heaven makes reply, —
"Take the cup cheerfully, drain the dregs fearlessly,
　　After life's bitterness, Death will tell *why*."

TWILIGHT MUSIC.

WHEN the swift December darkness
    Has hushed the sounds of mirth,
When the lamp is not yet lighted,
    But a flame is on the hearth,
Then let thy white hand wander
    Along the ivory keys,
With a touch as true and tender
    As the breath of twilight's breeze.

Not with the martial music
    That cheers the morning hour,
Not with the artist's rapture ·
    Of passion and of power;
But strains of old-time ballads,
    Hymns to the ages dear,
These are the speech of twilight
    That reach the spirit's ear.

Play on! this narrow chamber
  Takes form and aspect grand;
Yon darkened window opens
  Into a magic land,
As one by one they enter,
  And glide about the room, —
The shades of years departed
  Soft stealing through the gloom.

O Voice, still unforgotten,
  Why do I hear again
Thy mellow accent flowing
  In the sorrowful refrain?
O Face, that cometh never,
  Why in the firelight's glow
Dost thou gaze on me so wistful,
  With the look of long ago?

Play on! my spirit hearkens
  To numbers floating far;
My eyes no longer holden
  Look through the gates ajar.
There is no sound of voices,
  There is no rush of wings,
But in the twilight music
  A choir celestial sings.

THE SHADOW OF THE DAWN.

AT my first waking moment Sorrow came
   Beside my bed, and on my bosom laid
Her heavy hand; but I, grown less afraid
Since her first coming, uttered low a name
Mightier than hers, — and as the morning flame
   Burns from the valleys the miasmic shade,
   So that one word a sudden sunrise made
Within my soul, — and Sorrow fled in shame.

But ah! though that dear name has power to break
   The icy fetter laid upon my heart,
   And for each day's new service makes me free,
I know full well, that while I sleep or wake,
   Wan Sorrow never wholly will depart,
   But in the shadow lurks and watches me.

THE SUCCESSION.

AS one by one the singers of our land,
    Summoned away by death's unfailing dart,
  Unto the greater mystery depart,
Sadly we watch them from the desolate strand.
Oh! who shall fill their places in the band
    Of tuneful voices? Who with equal art
    Speak the unwritten language of the heart,
And the mute signs of Nature understand?

Yet poetry from earth has never ceased;
    It is a fire perpetual, which has caught
    Its flame from off the altar-place of Heaven.
Never has failed, in darkest days, a priest
    Who by no price of gain or glory bought,
    For his soul's peace his life to song has given.

THY SONG.

ASK me not which of all my songs is thine!
Ask of the Spring when first the blossoms stir
Which of their fairy pennons waves for her;
Ask of the Night what star of all that shine
Is her own signet, peerless and divine;
Ask of the Sun which purple follower
Among the clouds is his sole worshipper,
Lifting at dawn his colors and his sign.

As stars are born of night, as flowers of spring,
As clouds the vivid hues of sunlight wear,
And all an equal rank and kinship know,
So is thy memory the awakening,
The living warmth, the radiance large and fair
In which all songs of mine to utterance grow.

KLINGSOHR.

BY his low burning lamp at midnight hour,
Ulric the student read the ancient tale
Of Klingsohr, deathless King of Poesie.
He read that he it is who fires the brain
With thoughts of noble meaning, lights the soul
With splendid visions, and with voice that steals
The heart away leads upward to the stars.
If God or hero, spirit or living man,
Can no one say; he reigns invisible,
Content o'er hearts to hold eternal sway.
Once only, when a wild Hungarian king
Two noble minstrels would have slain because
Another's sounding measure pleased him more,
The magic Master strode into his court.

No robe of state he wore; his face was swarth
As one who holds free converse with the sun;
A peasant cloak of white hung round his knees;

Of hardy race and rustic life he seemed,
Yet in his eyes a fire celestial blazed ;
His attitude was kingly.   Every voice
Was mute with wonder, every breath was hushed,
While he made answer for the hapless bards.

"O King!" he spake, "lay not thy harmful hand
Upon these subjects of my realm!   Touch not
Their life nor freedom.   In thy narrow court
Slaves, courtiers, soldiers, tremble at thy frown ;
But empire such as thine cannot constrain
The worshippers of Beauty and of Song, —
Free souls are they and heirs of every clime.
Trouble not these who wear my royal seal, —
Klingsohr am I, of measureless domain."

Then turned he to the minstrels.   Sweet as dawn
The smile that lighted his majestic face,
And at his feet the singers fell and clasped
His shepherd garment, while the swift tears fell.
"Sing thou of love, and thou of war," he said,
"And both of beauty as ye read it best
In Nature's changing face.   There is no law
Nor limit to your freedom.   Human hearts
Alone your rank shall know, your crown shall weave."
This said he vanished, smiling as he passed,

And instantly a clangor of rich sounds,
A wonderful, entrancing melody,
All human passion glorified and changed
To heavenly adoration, through the air
Above them swept and ceased.　In ecstasy
The king and warriors stood with lifted eyes,
And from the silent court the bards went free.

As Ulric read, a sudden pulse of joy
Stirred all his being, the warm, midnight air
Throbbed audibly with mighty, moving wings,
And whether in his heart or at his ear
He knew not, but he heard a voice that said,
"Rise up, my brother, seek and follow me!"

Until the dawn the sleepless Ulric mused
Upon the path which he would early take
To find Klingsohr, henceforth his only liege.
"But have not many sought him?　I will go
First to the eldest, wisest of the bards,
He whose blue eyes of peace have longest looked
Upon the mountain-tops."　At break of day
He took his journey forth and sat at night
Beside the bard and told him his desire.
"I know Klingsohr," the Master said, and smiled
With gentle pity on the eager youth, —

" Know that he lives and reigns, the minstrel king,
And I have loved and served him loyally,
But seen him never.   Often has he sent
Heralds with trumpets, in the splendid dawn,
His coming to announce, or messengers
Who stole at night beside my wakeful bed,
In lute-tones delicate his wish to tell.
Then I, forgetting disappointments past,
Have risen in haste, have made a costly feast,
Brought wine of foreign vintage, treasured long
To place some day before his royal lips —
Then suddenly the herald music ceased,
The Master had passed by invisible,
And I, heart-sick and weary, could but taste
The costly viands, leaving still untouched
That which was rarest.   Yet I keep my house
Garnished and ready, lest some hour he come!"

The Poet's tale but fired young Ulric's zeal.
To seek the great magician, though by paths
Of bitter toil and hardships numberless,
To find him, make him visible but once,
And catch the measure of his mighty harp,
This seemed the only good that life could yield.
Long time he gave to study, sought rare books,
Records of many years and many climes,

Where oft, in mythic tales, he caught a glimpse
Of this song-master, but in none he found
The password to his secret dwelling-place.
He took long journeys, looking with keen eyes
Into men's faces, if perhaps some glance
Of majesty and beauty should reveal
The Ideal hidden in a human form.
But oh! at times how hopeless grew his quest!
So wrapped in narrow selfishness and greed
The clamoring crowd swept on.   Why longer seek?
How could the star-crowned walk these barren ways?
How could the song of songs in such a world
Ever one audible tone or word reveal?
But in such moments often would he hear
The striking of soft chords, prelusive notes
Of melody approaching, and again
He would make haste, and in swift, tremulous lines
Try to record the unreached harmony.

Along the highway one day flashed and passed
Long lines of horsemen and of infantry,
Brilliant in arms and tossing rainbow plumes,
In memory of some glorious victory.
And at their head rode one of statelier grace
Than all who followed.   He with piercing eyes
Looked upon Ulric as he passed and drew

Him onward with the magic of his gaze.
Then Ulric feeling that this warrior soul
At least was kindred to the king he sought,
Followed, and found a place to speak with him.

The warrior heard and answered musingly, —
" Klingsohr? I know him not, but I have heard
Majestic music on the battlefield,
Clearer than bugle, deeper than the drum,
Distinct above the battle's rage and roar, —
A wonderful, far-reaching melody
Which was not of the earth nor of the sky,
A thousand voices blended into one.
For Fatherland ! it rung — *for loyalty,*
For freedom, right, and endless good to man !
Oh, strong my heart within me grew, and strong
My right hand held the sword of victory,
Because that song resounded over me."

Stirred by the warrior's memories and full sure
That he was near the goal of his desire,
Ulric went on and sought the famous fields
Whereon this hero won his high renown.
But lo ! the hillsides swelled in velvet sward,
And all the trampled vales were sown with wheat,
And birds sprang shyly from their ground-built nests.

Awhile he lingered listening to the tales
Of war-worn veterans, but the sunlight keen,
The warm and waving branches and the thrill
Of nature's gladness, jarred with such a theme.
"He has gone hence," he sighed. "The battle-psalm
Delights him not in this sweet hour of peace.
The time is past when glory reigns alone
With kings and warriors. They who live for truth,
For honor and the universal weal,
Are dearer to the heart of Fatherland."

Straying he knew not whither, suddenly,
"Come hither! hither!" joyful voices cried,—
"To the rose-garden come and bring thy lute!"
And swift surrounding him a merry band
Of bright-haired youths and maidens led him on
Into a garden magical; for there
Grew blossoms never else together seen,
Young springtime and the autumn's richest prime
Blending their bloom and fragrance into one.
For there were banks of purple violet,
And arbutus, first whisper of the May,
And roses, choral of the summer dawn,
And honeysuckle, twilight kiss of love.
And there were water-lilies whose white cups
Brimmed with midsummer sweetness on the deeps

Of a still lake, and ripe autumnal flowers,
Arrayed like princesses of orient state,
Smiling and glowing from the terraces.

Then in a fairy-like, bewildering dance,
The lovers, clasping hands, flew o'er the green,
And Ulric, smitten with a new delight,
Played for them as they danced, then threw aside
His throbbing lute and sang with all his heart.
And as he sang, the dancers, one by one,
Looked in each other's eyes with tears of joy,
Drew close to him and sat about his feet;
And he, enraptured, heard a deep, soft sigh
Thrilling the air above him, and he poured
The story of a passion more divine
Then aught these lovers dreamed, and sang with might,
Believing that Klingsohr beside him stood,
With garment touching him invisibly.

But when the even came, the air grew chill,
The face which had been fairest turned away,
And Ulric rose and wandered through the grove,
Crushing the fallen roses as he called,
" Klingsohr! where art thou?   Show thy face to me!
Give me the song of love if not the joy! "

And from the sky behold there fell a star,
And on the wind funereal music sighed.

Then from the wilderness afar from men
Came deep Æolian whispers, and once more
The poet-pilgrim took his staff in hand.
" The dream of glory and of love is past !
In the still forest I will seek for him
Who has no need of worldly pomp or fame.
Somewhere in lodge invisible to sight
Of keenest hunter he serenely dwells,
Sweeping with loving touch the tremulous strings
Of Nature's never-silent instrument."

Then for full many days did Ulric dwell
Alone with Nature.   In a greenwood haunt
He gave himself to learning that deep speech
Which is the secret of all living things,
Whispered forever by the winds, the leaves
Of growing forests, and the murmuring brooks,
And understood and echoed by the birds, —
The ceaseless sigh and questioning of earth,
And Heaven's eternal, comforting response.

Here he had happy days, and scarcely felt
The pang of solitude, so sure he was
That he at last had reached the outer court

Of that great Presence he had sought so long.
For when the ever-blushing Dawn looked forth
From her rose-bordered window, he could hear
The sweet bells of the Day begin to chime;
He watched while Nature whispered in her dreams,
Stirred in her fragrant slumber, and arose
Trilling the prelude to a hymn of praise;
He learned to love the pæans of the storm,
To stretch forth arms of rapture when the winds
Held their wild wassail, or the white cascades
Leaped madly in their race for liberty
The inmost meaning of all forest lore
His rapt ear heard, his heart interpreted,
And yet the master key was unrevealed;
The word unutterable he strove to speak,
The face invisible he yearned to see.

And now the prime of summer days was past, —
A summer or a lifetime who can tell? —
When Ulric, sleeping, had a vision given.
He seemed to see a moving multitude
Hurrying each other, crowding to and fro,
Each seeking restlessly an unknown goal.
Before them silent and majestic walked
Klingsohr as once he trod the Eastern court,

A shepherd robe of white about his knees,
And an ineffable splendor on his face.

"Oh, why," the dreamer cried, "do they not seize
His hand, his garment's hem, and following him
Cease this bewildered, aimless wandering?"
But looking on them closer he perceived
Their eyes were holden and they could not see
The king before them.   Then with yearning strong
To tell them of the glory in their reach,
He woke.   From thence the charm of solitude
Was fled; he saw himself, with clearer eyes,
A dreamer in a world in need of men.
With quickened inspiration he went forth
To seek no longer for himself alone
The master of his destiny, Klingsohr.

As in the vision, quickly he perceived
That many sought in vain the true Ideal;
Brave youths, high-hearted maidens, hastened on,
Intent to reap the golden sheaves of life.
Faltering sometimes they asked, "Who is Klingsohr,
Whom we seek blindly, you by vision led?"
He answered with an ardor strong and new,
"He is the true, the lasting Victory!
He is the unattained, — yet not therefore

The unattainable, — and he who finds,
Has also found the pathway to the stars.
Let us go on in haste and hand in hand
In faithful brotherhood, for it may be,
The lowliest who is strong in loving zeal
May soonest see the Vision wonderful."
Thus filling their faint hearts with new desire,
Cheering, uplifting, strengthening, he went on,
And many joined the happy pilgrimage.

As birds return at spring to their old haunts,
Bringing the southland breezes on their wings,
So many wayside songs he once had sung
Came winging back to him, and many bore
A laurel-leaf and laid it on his brow.
And sweeter, tenderer with compassionate love,
And strong with heavenly prophecy, his words
Fell from the hard-won heights to vales below.

There came a day when on the mountain slope
Ulric, grown faint and weary, fell aside
From those who loved and followed him.   He heard
Their voices full of music and of cheer,
And gazed upon the banner beautiful
Borne in their midst, until it disappeared
As vanishes a crimson cloud at eve.

He was alone and yet not comfortless.
" At evening time it shall be light," he said,
And a great calm and peace possessed his soul.

Then all the western sky grew luminous,
The shining cloud-gates parted, and he saw
A grand, love-lighted face look out on him.
The shape grew large and lustrous, and a voice
Fell nearer, nearer, like a solemn bell,
Saying, "Arise and meet me! I am come!"

Then Ulric seeing that the goal was reached,
His life-work ended, uttered: " Ere I die,
Give me one measure of the song divine,
One true vibration from thy kingly harp!"
But Klingsohr answered: "I have been to thee
Close and perpetual comrade all thy way;
Myself I gave thee for thy knighthood true,
And these late laurel-leaves that garland thee
Are of my groves immortal. Yet forbear!
For ere thy hand upon my harp is laid,
And ere thou learn the theme of that high song
Which this world only echoes from above,
Thou must receive the sign and seal of death!"

Then Ulric sank down slowly, peacefully,
Heard once again the mighty, rushing wings,
Felt the ice-kiss of death upon his lips,
But saw, through all, the lofty, shining face.
And down the purple sunset hills there rolled
A river of majestic melody,
Love's utmost fervor, beauty's pure delight,
Triumph of hope, beatitude of praise,
Down flowing from the border-land of Day.
And his freed soul was lifted on that tide,
Uplifted and borne outward and away.

Thus had the pilgrim found at last Klingsohr;
Thus only had he learned the Song of Songs.

IN THE GARDEN.

WAS it thou, Mignonette?
       For while the south-wind stills its low complaints
To bear the censer of thy rich perfume,
I read, upon a terrace warm with bloom,
Flower-stories of the Virgin and the Saints.

I read that Mary, passing through a field,
Her heart oppressed with that mysterious gloom
Which ever falls on those whom Heaven has sealed
For glory's crown, — and doom, —
Paused often, in her meditative walk,
To pluck some favored blossom from its stalk,
Some happy flower, which bowed its beauteous head
And summer's odorous benediction shed.
       But one pale, scentless weed,
       Nor beautiful nor sweet,
       Which she would never heed,

But that it clung so close about her feet,
With tender touch she gathered: to her breast
And to her lips the fragile leaflets pressed,
Because so frail, so hopeless, loved the best!

Oh, then the poor weed strove
To whisper forth its rapture and its love!
And as it mutely trembled and adored,
Like praise of spirit risen
From long and woful prison,
A tide of fragrance from its heart was poured!

Nor once in all the ages has it sighed
For beauty's coronal of brilliant hue,
Red of the rose or violet's winsome blue,
By that one kiss of pity glorified.
The garden's lowly, well-beloved flower,
A miracle of sweetness from that hour, —
Mignonette, was it thou?

ALCYONE.

I.

AMONG the thousand, thousand spheres that roll,
  Wheel within wheel, through never-ending space,
A mighty and interminable race,
Yet held by some invisible control,
And led as to a sure and shining goal,
One star alone with still, unchanging face,
Looks out from her perpetual dwelling-place,
Of these swift orbs the centre and the soul.

Beyond the moons that beam, the suns that blaze,
Past fields of ether, crimson, violet, rose,
The vast star-garden of eternity,
Behold! it shines with white, immaculate rays,
The home of peace, the haven of repose,
The lotus-flower of heaven, Alcyone.

II.

IT is the place where life's long dream comes true:
On many another swift and radiant star
Gather the flaming hosts of those who war
With powers of Darkness; those strong seraphs too
Who hasten forth God's ministries to do;
But here no sounds of eager trumpets mar
The subtler spell which calls the soul from far,
Its wasted springs of gladness to renew.

It is the morning land of the Ideal,
Where smiles, transfigured to the raptured sight,
The joy whose flitting semblance now we see;
Where we shall know as visible and real
Our life's deep aspiration, old yet new
In the sky splendor of Alcyone.

III.

WHAT lies beyond we ask not.   In that hour
When first our feet that shore of beauty press,
It is enough of heaven, its sweet success,
To find our own.   Not yet we crave the dower
Of grander action and sublimer power;
We are content that life's long loneliness
Finds in love's welcoming its rich redress,
And hopes, deep hidden, burst in perfect flower.

Wait for me there, O loved of many days!
Though with warm beams some beckoning planet glows,
Its dawning triumphs keep, to share with me;
For soon, far winging through the starry maze,
Past fields of ether, crimson, violet, rose,
I follow, follow, to Alcyone!